# THE BURNING TREE

## STAZ

Dedicated to anyone who finds the straight and narrow path, no matter where they may have started from.

# CONTENTS

# PROLOGUE

Looking back, I can hardly believe that it even happened. But that was another time, another place, back when I was a completely different girl. It was the time I had nearly lost myself in wind cleansings, brutal competitions, and the fury of grown men who had free rein to abuse young girls, all in the name of religion.

It's difficult to understand how something like "The Community" could happen in modern times in the United States. But as my counselor tells me, if all the ingredients are there; isolation from mainstream society, coercion, threats, and above all, a charismatic leader, unfortunately, people often fall victim to cults.

But no one who lived there ever thought of it as a cult, at least not until the end, until the time we were trying to escape. We'd been so blinded by fear and false authority that what was beyond imaginable had to happen before our eyes were opened, and we finally saw the truth.

"Hannah... Hannah," the counselor says, bringing me out of the daze I've fallen into. It happens so often now. My mind wanders, thoughts grow fuzzy, and I see the eyes of Hayden McVeigh, as white as ice.

"Hannah, you were telling me about the punishment, the wind cleansing," the counselor says, her voice soft and gentle this time.

I nod, trying to remember where I am. This is the third time in two weeks I've told her the whole story. Each time I go through it, I remember a little more – and each time, I'm more frightened by what I hear myself say.

I open my mouth, and words pour out like quicksand. I hold onto the arms of the chair, afraid that I'll drown in the sound of my own voice. My new pastor says that God will not allow more to happen to me than I can bear. That's probably why I only remember the last year at the Community in bits and pieces. If it flooded into conscious thought all at once, it would probably destroy me.

The counselor is typing into a laptop while the tape recorder runs silently on the table. And as I hear myself speak, I'm listening to the voice of that other girl, the one whose bones I dig up every time I retell this nightmare. But my counselor says I have to dig her up, piece by piece. I have to remember who she is before I can figure out who I am.

# Chapter One

The Wyoming wind blew in bitter cold from the Laramie Mountains, withering the last of the remaining plants and grass into tiny bristles. Only the bony stems of the sagebrush survived, picking up bits of dirt while rolling across the barren landscape.

I rotated my shoulders in a feeble attempt to relieve the aching muscles in my neck, but the way my arms were tied to the poles made the effort useless. The sustained thirty-mile-per-hour wind was almost unbearable, and my lips and cheeks, which had chapped hours earlier, were starting to crack and bleed. I didn't dare open my mouth or eyes. The dry, frozen bits of dust and dirt would sting like tiny shards of broken glass.

The elders usually gave punishments that involved nature. *Cleansing by the elements – wind, water, and earth – will cleanse the soul*, Elder McVeigh always said.

Anything that didn't have to do with nature or physical activity was viewed with suspicion and often considered evil. That was why when I had been caught by an elder's wife listening to an iPod and, of all things, rock and roll music, I was sentenced to a wind cleansing.

Eight hours earlier, I'd been brought to an open field and had my wrists tied to two wooden posts spaced three feet apart. I was at just the precise height that I couldn't stand straight, but neither could I rest on my knees. It was a horrible position for the joints and muscles of the lower back. The rack would have been a mercy.

Once a thin layer of snow had coated the ground, I could finally open my eyes without worrying about the burning dust and dirt. I tilted my head back, letting the moisture cover my face. The soft, fluffy snow melted in my mouth, soothing my chapped, cracked lips. Blood mingled with the snow, but I didn't care. I was so thirsty that I gulped it down as soon as it melted.

But relief in the form of snow was temporary. The temperature was dropping rapidly, and the density of the snow was constantly increasing. January in Wyoming could be brutal, and the weather could turn from mild to vicious in a relatively short time. If I had to remain outside much longer, I could easily freeze to death.

*Run away, into my arms, into the night... Give me all your love; it's more than all right.*

These were the words of Sandstone Pilot, a twenty-year-old punk rock musician and a sure messenger of the devil according to the elders.

*Burn, burn in hell... God may never forgive; you've gone too far, and only with purification do you stand a chance.*

The words of Hayden McVeigh, stern-faced elder and self-appointed prophet of God. Both voices screamed at one another in my head.

The next time I looked up, Hayden McVeigh and Jonathon Alden were trudging toward me through the blinding snow. Almost simultaneously, each one snapped open a pocketknife and cut the ropes around my wrists. I would have fallen face-first into the snow if they hadn't each grabbed an arm.

"Had enough?" Jonathon Alden said, his powerful voice breaking through the wind.

My throat had already been ravaged by the cold, and nothing came out but a weak moan. I barely had the strength to hold on while they dragged me to the van.

There were only two vehicles in a community of over two hundred people, and both belonged to elders Hayden McVeigh and Jonathon Alden. In the quest for the simple, natural life, a van and a pickup truck had been purchased for the rare trip outside of *the Community*.

Jonathon opened the back double doors of the large cargo van while Hayden picked me up and slid me inside. The warmth cradled my aching body, and I began to sigh out of relief.

Both men climbed in the front, and Jonathon started the engine. By the time the van was on the main road of the Community, my fingers and toes had gone from numb to unbearable pain.

Set back from the main road, on both sides, were dozens of white, rectangular homes. They were small, resembling homes sharecroppers would live in, with no more than three or four rooms. But they were built sturdy to withstand the harsh Wyoming winters.

The van stopped in front of house #14, and I was pulled from the back. While Hayden McVeigh held me up, Jonathon Alden knocked on my mother's front door. When she saw me, decimated by wind, cold, and the wrath of the Community elders, she started to gasp but quickly brought her emotions under control.

"The process is complete," Jonathan Alden stated plainly.

My mother was standing perfectly still, but I could see her hands trembling.

"I'm sorry, Mrs. Sawyer, but it was for her own good," Hayden McVeigh said as he leaned down toward me. "There won't be any need for more discipline, will there now?"

I slowly shook my head. He picked me up, carried me to the sofa, and left me watching their backs as they plodded out of our home.

When the door closed, my mother pulled a blanket out from under the sofa and tucked it under my chin. "You've known since you were a little girl the consequences of using phones, televisions, computers, or anything electronic and unnatural."

I opened my mouth and tried to tell her about the amazing little machine, how people came to sing and dance in my head just by pushing a tiny plug into my ear.

But she put a finger to her lips before the words could crawl through my raw throat. "No," she whispered. "Don't even say it. It's against God and all that's decent."

She stood up and walked away, shaking her head when she stopped at the window.

"Elizabeth McVeigh found it and destroyed it," she said, staring out at the horizon, now melted into a blinding wash of snow.

She came back and gently began rubbing my wrists, which were aching from the sting of rope burns. Despite what I'd just been through, I couldn't help but think about that amazing little machine called an iPod. Since I'd turned 16 several months earlier, I'd increasingly been thinking about the many things in life that lay beyond the borders of the Community.

"Who gave that thing to you?" my mother asked, breaching her own code of silence. "It was Alison, wasn't it? They thought they'd break her if they got her here in time. But fifteen is too late. And that girl is nothing but trouble."

"Mother," I whispered. I reached up to my lips. They were bleeding again in the warmth of the house.

"I'll get something for that," she said nervously.

She came back with a jar of Vaseline. Reaching deep into the jar, she scooped it out two fingers at a time and applied a thick layer to my lips and cheeks.

She started talking again. This time, she talked about the stove not working properly, about Jada Brewer's latest bout with the flu, about everything, yet nothing at all. Maybe, so

I wouldn't talk, or maybe because she couldn't help herself anymore.

Then she took a deep breath, choking down what sounded like crying. She had to let it out, and there was no one else to tell except me. I could only remember my mother talking about why we came here a few times since we arrived eight years earlier. But this time was different. It was more of a confession than an explanation.

"Life wasn't always like this," my mother said, barely above a whisper. "I still remember the Sunday Hayden and Elizabeth McVeigh came to our church in Denver. They put the fear of the devil into anyone who wouldn't drop everything right then and there and follow them to Wyoming to start a new life."

She leaned over and scooped out the Vaseline again, this time spreading it over the top of my hands and wrists.

"Why did you come? Why did you follow them here?" I said, forcing out the words.

She squeezed her eyes shut and then slowly opened them. "Your father was so sick. He had fourth-stage pancreatic cancer, and the doctors had all but given up hope."

She hesitated, taking a deep breath to keep from crying. I was eight years old when all this happened, but for some reason, I was barely able to remember any of it. Perhaps it was because my dad had seemed so robust and strong, even up to the end. Or maybe it was because I'd never wanted to leave the life we'd had in Denver, all my friends, my school, and the great neighborhood we lived in.

"Hayden McVeigh told us that if he came to Wyoming and lived the natural life, free from all the toxins and pollutants, and away from all the evil that plagued the city, he would be healed."

She smiled, probably remembering the hope she'd had at that time, the hope they'd all had.

"They built this place, twenty miles northwest of Wheatland, about as far from civilization as a person could get without leaving the continental United States. To get any further from mainstream society, a person would have to travel to the Amazon rainforest or the mountains of Afghanistan. But that was how Hayden McVeigh and Jonathon Alden had wanted it when they pooled their followers' money and bought over seventy acres of Wyoming wilderness."

Then the smile melted off her face as she remembered how all of her grand hopes for our future in the Community had died along with her husband.

"Why didn't we go back to Denver after Dad died?" I insisted.

"We gave the McVeighs and the Aldens all we had when we came here; everyone did. Bank accounts, cashed-out retirement funds, and even houses and cars were sold so we could buy this property, the animals, and all the materials needed to build the Community."

And then she smiled again. "And, of course, I had a baby to care for then," she said, referring to my little sister, Abigail.

"What about the others? What about the Watsons, the Flowers, and the rest? Why did they come?"

"Oh, different reasons, I suppose. It sounded so good then, natural living based on biblical principles and getting away from the turmoil of what had become our modern civilization. But somewhere along the way, things changed."

She ran her fingers over my face and lips, smoothing the Vaseline into a thin layer.

"Jada Brewer was a widow who thought Hayden McVeigh had been sent from God Himself to rescue her from poverty and loneliness. Steve and Amy Flowers came later because their older children had become so rebellious, falling into drugs and a bad crowd. And the rest, I don't know for sure. I'm certain they all had their reasons for coming."

She got up after that and went into the kitchen to fix me something to eat. When I could smell the thick aroma of chicken soup on the stove, I lay back on the sofa and closed my eyes. Everything would be alright. I would do better, everything the elders wanted me to do. I convinced myself I had so much to look forward to during the next few months.

The Preparation would be starting soon, and things would be different. I forced myself to believe it like I'd done so many times before. While I was trying to imagine exactly what my role in the Preparation would be, my nine-year-old sister, Abigail, opened the front door and came running toward me.

"Hannah, you're back!" she cried. She jumped on the sofa beside me and threw her arms around me.

As she pressed against my body, the pain was excruciating, but I was so happy to see her that I let her wrap her arms around my aching shoulders.

"Are you okay?" she asked, finally letting go.

I just couldn't let her know how horrible it had been. "Yes," I said.

"Go get cleaned up," my mother ordered Abigail. "Let your sister eat."

"Sure," she said, backing out of the room, never taking her eyes off me. She had probably been terrified the night they dragged me away, crying and pleading. She'd probably been afraid I might not come back. After all, I'd been afraid of that myself.

# Chapter Two

Two weeks later:

Hayden McVeigh towered over the tiny girls like one of the massive oaks that lined the eastern woods. When he lifted the pistol above his head, I thought how frightening and powerful he looked. But even a gun was no match for the pulpit. He still held more power when he stood behind a wooden frame preaching hellfire and damnation than at the end of the main road with his finger on the trigger.

"On your marks... get set..."

*Bang!*

As soon as the gun went off, the gravel flew beneath bare feet, and the entire group of little girls took off racing toward the front of the general store. Jonathan Alden stood at the other end of the main road while each girl struggled to reach the finish line first. Between Jonathon and seven nervous little girls stood the Community Hall, the sanctuary, the general store, and exactly one hundred yards of gravel, mud, and slushy snow.

"Go, Abigail!" I cried. My voice had returned to normal since the wind cleansing but was still drowned out by at least a dozen others cheering for someone from their own family.

The littlest girls past the age of accountability always started off the competitions each Saturday morning. I watched anxiously as their small legs beat into the dust, dirt, and snow. They appeared to be running and dancing at the same time. Each race was a choice between running as fast as possible without regard to the obstacles purposely placed along the road or looking for and side-stepping potentially dangerous objects.

Jagged stones and twigs with sharpened edges placed along the road as inconspicuously as possible forced runners to make a terrible choice. Sometimes, even glittering shards of glass were put along the running path. During the summer, it was easier to avoid these obstacles. In the winter, glass was nearly impossible to see in the ice and snow.

Winning was not only about being the fastest and the strongest but about being able to dodge obstacles and sometimes even endure torturous pain. I didn't care if my little sister won or lost any race, only that she made it to the finish line without any injuries.

Abigail would be lucky today. She would make it across this entire stretch of the main road without stepping on a single twig or pebble. But before anyone had crossed the finish line, Melissa Smyth had the misfortune of landing on a fragment of glass, a rock perhaps; I wasn't sure. About forty yards into the race, she crumpled to the ground, close to where I was standing. From where I was, it didn't look as if anything had penetrated her foot.

Nevertheless, she howled with pain as she fell into a ball on the main road. No one ran to her rescue. It was not permitted. I could see her mother standing stiffly near the front steps of the Community Hall. Her father's hand grasped her forearm as if he was holding her back. The other girls finished the race without incident, without looking back, and without stopping.

Jonathon Alden was at the far end of the road, meticulously recording the names of the winners and losers in the Community book. It was Hayden McVeigh's duty to deal with Melissa Smyth. His slow, steady pace indicated that he was in no hurry. He stopped a few feet away from where she was lying and leaned over, casting an enormous shadow over her trembling body.

He pointed a finger and declared, "We'll have no crying! The weak and the cowardly are an abomination to God! Now get up immediately."

"It hurts too much!" she cried, burying her face in her hands. She rocked back and forth while clutching her foot, her curly blonde hair wet and matted against her face. As she turned away from Elder McVeigh, the bottoms of her feet turned along with her, and it could easily be seen that she was not seriously injured. Without excessive amounts of blood or broken bones, there would be no mercy.

"Bring the Word of God!" Hayden McVeigh cried.

Hayden's wife, Elizabeth, retrieved the large Bible that was always kept near the Community book. Hayden quickly found the verse he was searching for. He looked down at Melissa while reading, but the words were loud enough that the entire Community could hear.

*If thou faint in the day of adversity, thy strength is small.*

Proverbs 24:10

He read the words evenly as she struggled like a wounded animal to stand. If she wasn't standing before he finished, the Bible would be closed, and judgment passed. She had only a few seconds, and Hayden McVeigh was not a patient man.

Her legs were long and gangly, like a baby colt not long after birth. Somehow, she managed to stand before Elder McVeigh had finished. On the table near the finish line, Jonathon Alden was writing furiously in the Community book. It was large and leather-bound, with thick pages. Jonathon stared at Melissa Smyth with disdain while continuing to write.

"This is a good day for Abigail," my friend Katie whispered.

I nodded without looking back. Being a winner meant that others must lose. In Abigail's case, a glowing report written in the book came at the expense of another little girl. It was brutal to hope for such misery on one another, but it was a matter of survival, and I couldn't let myself worry about Melissa Smyth when my little sister's well-being was at stake.

But Melissa's shame would quickly be forgotten. There were two more age groups for the girls, and then each of the boys' races would be run. It was unlikely that the remaining races would be run without someone stumbling or injuring themselves beyond their ability to endure.

Hayden McVeigh walked back to the end of the main street, cradling the gun in his hands. "We need the 11 to 14 year-olds!" he announced.

There were only five girls in this particular group this year. The race was completed without incident, and the winners' and losers' names were recorded in the book.

It was now time for the girls in the Preparation. Katie walked with me to the starting line. There were several other girls in our age group who would be running as well. None of us looked at each other, spoke, or even acknowledged one another once we had been called.

As Hayden McVeigh waited impatiently for us to take off our shoes and socks and line up parallel to the water tank, Jonathan Alden stood at the far end of the main street, waiting for us to run toward him as if our lives depended on it. While the elders were intently watching us, I watched Patrick and Robbie McVeigh. As soon as I slipped off my faded tennis shoes and dirty socks, I saw them at the other end of the road.

Robbie was Hayden's unmarried oldest son. He was considered a junior elder in training and demanded almost as much respect as an elder. He was also a terror to all the teenage girls in the Community. He would make rude comments that none of the other adults seemed to hear and purposely rub against us when passing by, even if there was plenty of room not to. Patrick McVeigh was Hayden's married, much younger brother and was a hundred times worse.

"On your marks!"

Every girl was lined up, shoulder to shoulder, each of us hunched over like tigers, ready to lurch.

"Get set!"

Robbie and Patrick stood at the finish line, smiling, waiting for us to run to them.

*"Bang!"*

I started running faster than I'd ever run before, hoping I'd run right into one of them, knocking them down so hard they'd never get back up again. When I sensed someone coming up next to me, I temporarily forgot about Patrick and Robbie and attempted to lengthen my stride, pump my fists, and finally win the hundred-yard dash. But it was no use. Alison was at least two inches taller and had legs that stretched like a deer in flight.

When I finally finished, I turned around and watched the other girls. I was in second place. Not bad, considering that at least half the time Whitney beat me, and sometimes even Adalei managed to squeeze by at the last second.

Thankfully, everyone made it across the finish line without any trouble. As soon as I caught my breath, I looked around for Patrick and Robbie. But they were gone.

The boys' races started almost immediately after Jonathon had finished recording the results for the girls. The youngest boys were followed by those in the 11 to 14 age group. Finally, the boys in the Preparation were called to line up.

It was the last 100-yard dash before we would move on to the other competitions. The gun went off, and the boys began to run, each of their faces stern with determination. As serious as physical fitness and stamina were for girls, this was held in even higher regard for boys.

It looked as if nothing serious would transpire during the dashes today – nothing more than a little girl who fell but managed to get up before anything terrible could happen. And then, as quickly as that thought rolled through my mind, Terrance O'Malley's legs gave way beneath him, and he came crashing to the ground.

This time, the crying was different, more unbearable than the cries from Melissa Smyth. It was an agonizing, blood-curdling scream that sounded like one born of madness and not just pain. Within seconds, the ground where the boy lay was filled with blood.

Elder McVeigh walked close enough to evaluate Terrance's situation and then made a quick motion in Jonathon Alden's direction. Jonathon promptly sent his wife to find Ruth Anne Weber, the Community nurse and midwife.

Of course, Ruth Anne was already in the crowd. The entire Community came out to watch the competitions. And she had certainly seen the spectacle that was Terrance O'Malley screaming in pain in the middle of the main road. But she couldn't do anything about it without permission from the elders.

As soon as permission was given, Ruth Anne called for two men to carry Terrance to her medical office behind her home, where she could examine and then tend to the large shard of glass that had penetrated the ball of his left foot. The moment he had been carried away, several men arrived with shovels and rakes.

The ground where Terrance had bled profusely was dug up and turned over several times. Fresh dirt was raked over the top. Everything was now spotless and new as if it had never happened.

# Chapter Three

Several teenagers in the Community were going through the Preparation. In my age group, five girls had been chosen to work and train together through the transition from adolescence into official adulthood.

Alison Flowers had only been here a little over a year, was the oldest, and had the most experience in the outside world. She would say things that shocked the rest of us. She'd talk about sex and try to make jokes about things none of us had even heard of or understood. When she started talking like that, we'd look at each other like she was speaking a foreign language.

Lynette Brewer, whose family had lived in a complex with the McVeigh family before they started the Community, had been sheltered from the reality of modern life since she'd been a baby. She'd never seen a computer or talked on a phone.

Katie Watson and I came from Denver in the third grade. We seemed to have a connection I hadn't formed with anyone else in the Community, and we spent as much time together as possible.

Whitney Crouse was also our age and in our group, but I didn't know much about her. She had six younger brothers and sisters and was often required to leave the group to help her mother care for them.

Our time together was usually spent doing chores or participating in group training sessions with the older women. By age 15, formal schooling was finished, and we were groomed for adulthood through a process that had been named "The Preparation."

The Preparation consisted of everything from learning a particular skill to how to dress for our future husbands and care for children. Our group was also required to clean the Community Hall twice a week and gather sticks and firewood for all the wood-burning stoves that kept the Community warm.

After the competitions were over and we had finished our weekly Community dinner, the five of us started walking down the main road, a crisp wind at our backs. I quickly buttoned up my denim jacket and stuffed my hands into my oversized overall pockets, which was the Community "uniform" for those – male and female – who hadn't officially reached adulthood.

"What happened to Terrance? How bad is he hurt?" I said, looking in Lynette's direction. Her grandmother, Jada Brewer, was an expert at growing and mixing medicinal herbs. Any medicine for Terrance would have come from Jada and Lynette's home.

Lynette shrugged. "No one came to our house asking Grandma to make anything. Ruth Anne must have had enough."

"They didn't use any medicine," Alison said. "No painkillers or anything. And I know it because my dad was working on the Weber's roof while Ruth Anne was tending to him."

"Why wouldn't they use anything?" I asked softly. I was afraid of the answer.

"My dad heard the elders telling Terrance how he acted when he got injured was disgraceful and not acceptable for a Community man. Then they told him they would erase it all from the book if he took his treatment without pain medication."

Katie's eyes grew large with anticipation. "Did he agree?"

We had all slowed down to the point that we were barely walking, each of us waiting to find out what happened to Terrance O'Malley.

But Alison only shrugged. "My dad left before he could find out for sure."

"He probably took the pain," Lynette said. "No one came to our house for any kind of medication."

"They might have had some left over," I said.

"At any rate, we'll probably never know, at least not until we find out everyone's ranking in the book when it comes time to pick marriage partners," Alison said. "They keep the Community book locked up tighter than gold at Fort Knox."

"What's Fort Knox?" Lynette asked.

Alison looked at her like she'd just asked what two plus two was.

As much as I also wanted to know what Fort Knox was, I knew we had to get busy gathering wood. We were required to fill two wheelbarrows as full as possible. It was going to be a cold night. Between the two largest barns were wheelbarrows and a storage container full of gardening equipment and tools. Alison and I each began pushing a wheelbarrow while Lynette, Whitney, and Katie followed close behind.

At the edge of the Community, where the main gravel road ended in a grassy meadow, we saw Patrick standing by the last animal barn. He was kneeling, repairing the chicken wire around the hen house.

Patrick McVeigh had a body like a seasoned Olympic weightlifter who'd spent his entire life building each muscle until it couldn't expand any further. From the neck down, he was well-proportioned; some might even say beautiful, like a statue that had been carefully sculpted. From the neck up, he was something else entirely different. His eyes were white; even the pupils were pale and yellowish, and his skin was pasty like dried glue.

"He is attractive," Alison said after we had passed him and were heading into the field and toward the woods.

Lynette looked mortified. "He's married. And he's old."

"He's not that old," Alison countered, which made me laugh.

When I saw the look on Katie's face, I knew I shouldn't have. Her eyes filled with fear at the very mention of Patrick's name. Of course, we all thought the way he acted toward the single girls was nothing short of disgusting, but fear was not something I'd ever felt up to that point.

"He's got to be at least thirty-five," Lynette said.

"Thirty-four," Alison replied.

How she knew exactly how old Patrick McVeigh was, I had no idea. I probably would have asked if I hadn't been so concerned about Katie.

Alison led the way toward the thickest section of the woods, with Lynette and Whitney behind her. Katie fell back, several yards behind us. I slowed down until I was next to her.

"I know neither of us can stand Patrick, but something is upsetting you more than usual," I said.

I could tell she was breathing heavier, as if it took all her energy to concentrate on keeping the air moving in and out of her lungs. But she didn't say anything for several seconds. I waited patiently, walking quietly beside her.

"He won't leave me alone," she finally said, her voice barely above a whisper so the others couldn't hear.

I knew what he had tried to do to Lynette a few months earlier when she had been alone in the general store. She had managed to get away from him when her grandmother came in unexpectedly. My heart was racing as I asked, "What exactly has happened?"

"He... he touches me... in places he shouldn't."

I felt a chill run through my body. I knew he was overly flirtatious and would "accidentally" bump into us whenever he had a chance. But I didn't think he would touch a girl in such a blatant and obvious way.

"He's married. Maybe it wasn't on purpose," I said, trying to make myself believe it.

"I don't know how to stop him," Katie said, her voice a whimper.

I stopped walking. "When does this happen? When does he get you alone?"

She sighed. "When I'm walking home after chores or races, just any time there's even a few seconds when no one else is around."

Lynette turned and looked over her shoulder. "Are you two coming?"

I grabbed the wheelbarrow handles and we started walking again, both of us staring intently at our feet pounding into the icy ground. I was suddenly at a loss for words, and our silence was awkward. But I had never known Katie to lie about anything, not even exaggerating.

"Do you believe me?" she asked.

I didn't want to believe her. I tried to come up with some plausible reason why I knew she was mistaken. But I couldn't. "Yes," I said. "I believe you."

By the time we came to the edge of the woods, we methodically began picking up sticks. The sticks were to be at least a foot long and approximately a half-inch thick, the perfect size for kindling and keeping the fire-burning stoves in each of our homes lit throughout the night.

I bent down and picked one up, making sure not to grab more than one at a time. I bent down again and picked up another. We each had our own rhythm that we stayed in time with.

Our arms were nearly full when Lynette tilted her head back and gazed at the smoke hovering above us. Fires were almost constantly burning in the Community for either cooking or heat, so seeing smoke was not unusual.

But where the fire seemed to be coming from, about a quarter mile to the east, where there was a vast meadow and a cluster of trees, was quite a distance from the edge of the Community. It wasn't until the flames were shooting up towards the tops of the trees that we finally saw this massive blaze, now sprawling almost an acre wide.

"Look!" Katie cried, pointing a finger.

There wasn't much wind, but the air was dry, and stubble and parched grass in the meadow burned as if it had been sparked by kerosene.

"All those trees are on fire," I said.

Lynette turned around and spoke in the direction of the flames. "We need to tell someone before it spreads any further."

The rest of us nodded in agreement, but no one moved. For what seemed like a long time, we stood there staring in amazement, mesmerized by the flames.

Alison started to turn and was about to run back toward the Community when Lynette grabbed her arm. "It's probably the witches," she said.

We all looked at her at the same time. According to the elders, a group of witches had moved into a cluster of abandoned cabins about half a mile past the north meadow. They told us the witches practiced black magic and conjured up dark spells, receiving their power from the devil himself.

We stared in the direction of the cabins, watching the fire as it continued to spread toward us. We might have stayed there all night if it had not been for the dark smoke circling over our heads, grayish tentacles finally reaching down and filling our lungs.

"Come on, we have to go back," Katie said.

# Chapter Four

It took almost four hours for the Platte County Fire Department to get the blaze under control. That's what the fire chief said when he came to the McVeigh house, still wearing the yellow and black fire uniform, now drenched with the heavy smell of smoke.

Eleven girls between the ages of fifteen and seventeen were sitting around the kitchen table, needle and thread in hand, perfecting a cross stitch while Elder McVeigh and the fire chief talked in the next room. Elizabeth McVeigh continued to walk in circles around the table, hovering over each of us, reaching in and correcting whenever we made the smallest mistake. Her eyes were small and narrow, but they were quick to catch an uneven stitch or sloppy needlework.

We were all looking down, pretending to be enamored with sewing a dish towel by hand. But we were hanging on every word of the conversation in the living room, quiet as mice, eager for information anyone outside of the Community might bring us. This was only the second time I could ever remember seeing another human being from the outside visit the Community.

The first had been several years earlier when a doctor had been summoned to deliver Elizabeth McVeigh's fifth child, a baby that had been born breech and had nearly caused his mother to bleed to death.

Lowell Meyer, the county fire chief, coughed and cleared his throat. "After I took a good look at all the destruction out there, I could hardly believe what I saw."

From where I was sitting in the kitchen, I couldn't see Lowell Meyer, but I saw Hayden McVeigh, dressed in overalls and a deerskin jacket, keeping a cautious distance from the fire chief, a stranger – not one of us.

"Do you own that meadow that burned?" Meyer asked.

"We all own it," Elder McVeigh said stiffly. "The Community owns it."

"Awfully dry out there. Sometimes those things start on their own," Meyer said.

I could hear the sound of his heavy steps as he walked toward the window. When I finally got a glimpse of him, I was surprised by how young and handsome he was for a fire chief.

Elder McVeigh shook his head. "That witches' coven, about half a mile past the north field, wouldn't be surprised one bit if they started it."

"Witches' coven?" Meyer scratched his head and then looked out the window as if the witches might be out there in plain sight. "I don't know of any witches' coven anywhere in this area."

"We think they're staying in those old cabins right past the north meadow," Elder McVeigh said. He frowned and shook his head. "Rumor has it they kill animals to sacrifice to the devil. They have chemicals they add to the fire to make it burn hotter."

I didn't hear the fire chief say anything for a few seconds, and I knew he was trying to figure out what to make of all these accusations of animal sacrifice and devil worship.

"We have patrols that check those abandoned cabins every so often. We haven't seen any unusual activity around there in years. And I haven't heard anything about any witches, but we'll do the usual investigation and see what we find," he finally said.

Elder McVeigh nodded. "If that's all, you can show yourself out." He walked away without saying as much as a thank you to the fire department for putting out a fire that came close to where we lived.

The truth was, the county fire department had not been called, nor had their services been wanted. Community men had worked half the night with buckets of water and shovels digging ravines to keep the fire from spreading into the Community.

A fire of that magnitude, however, garners attention even when society is miles away. When it became obvious that modern methods would be needed to contain the fire, the Community men left the remainder of the job to Lowell Meyer and his firefighters.

I couldn't see where Elder McVeigh had gone, but I could hear the steady clip-clopping of his heavy boots. The fire chief, in his bright yellow uniform, stood in the living room for a few seconds before leaving. I leaned forward slightly, mesmerized by what he was doing.

He pulled out a tiny black object, which I knew was a cell phone. I could vaguely remember using one. I knew the elders carried them for emergencies and had seen them on occasion. I listened with amazement as he tapped in the numbers. Beep, beep, beep, beep... He turned and walked toward the front door.

"I'll be home in about twenty minutes," I heard him say into the magical device. A few seconds later, he disappeared from view, and his voice faded away.

I must have been staring too long, not watching my work, and being a "busybody" as I gazed into the next room. And even though I could stitch well enough that I didn't have to look down constantly, Elizabeth McVeigh made sure I would never be into someone else's business again while tending to my work. In a split second, she grabbed hold of my left hand and slammed it down hard on the needle that I held in my right hand.

Everything instantly went dark. I blacked out for a second or two, but not enough time to pass out. As soon as the stars in my eyes dissipated, I felt a sharp, searing pain race through the palm of my hand. I heard at least one of the girls scream. I think it was Lynette. Thankfully, all conscious thought finally melted into blackness, and I temporarily passed out. Seconds later, lying crumpled over the kitchen table, I came to and let out a horrific scream. Then I began crying like a small child.

Later, I'd find out that only Lynette immediately saw what happened and had screamed even before I did. The rest of the girls gasped in horror when they saw what had happened, but quickly composed themselves before Elizabeth McVeigh could punish them as well.

"It's not your business to pay attention to what the men are doing," Elizabeth ordered, sticking her face so close to mine I could feel her hot breath.

I'm not sure how I had the presence of mind to pull the needle out, but I instinctively did. Then the blood swelled, and my crying subsided, melting into slow, hiccupy sobs. Hayden McVeigh glanced into the kitchen, looked down at the bloody table, and then walked outside.

Elizabeth opened a drawer and retrieved a clean dishcloth. She wrapped the towel around my hand and instructed me to soak the wound in iodine when I got home.

"Now stop your whining. There'll be worse pain than that when you become a proper wife and mother." She stomped over to the sink and rinsed my blood off her hands. She didn't bother to offer me a wet towel or even any water. "Women must learn to suffer properly and with dignity."

I was permitted to leave, not because Elizabeth McVeigh pitied me or worried that the wound might become infected if not cleaned immediately, but because my hand was bleeding through the dish towel she had wrapped around it.

Elizabeth's kitchen was sparse, but it was neat and clean, with nothing out of order. Splatters of blood on a freshly scrubbed wooden table were considered intolerable. And so I was promptly sent home. Before leaving the kitchen, the embroidered dish towel I had been working on was discarded, and I was told I would have to work extra hours making a new one.

None of the other girls would make eye contact as I left. It made me angry they had abandoned me, but I couldn't blame them.

I was only able to take two or three steps at a time before stopping and taking a deep breath to ease the pain. It seemed to take forever just to get out of the house and onto the road.

When I was far enough away from the McVeigh house that I knew Elizabeth could no longer watch me from the front window, I stopped along the side of the road. Bending down carefully, I picked up a handful of snow with my other hand and quickly stuffed it under the towel before any blood could escape. The thick, icy snow felt wonderful, and for a few moments, the throbbing subsided.

By the time I was home, and the heat from the front room had engulfed me, the snow melted into the blood and the torn flesh, and the searing pain again took root and sprouted through my entire arm. I stood just a few feet inside our living room, taking slow, deep breaths, thankful I was finally home.

My mother was in the kitchen preparing large quantities of potato soup for the next Community gathering. She didn't seem to notice that I had come home, and I tried to make it to the bathroom before she saw me.

When the bleeding started getting heavier in the warmth of the house and began to drip on our clean floor, I grabbed hold of the wound and attempted to press it so it would stop. I tripped, and my mother suddenly looked up and saw me awkwardly staggering toward the bathroom.

"What happened?" she said, quickly looking over her shoulder to see if Abigail was paying attention. Abigail was in the kitchen measuring the flour that was to go into the potato soup.

"I wasn't paying attention to my work. And Elizabeth..."

Abigail was now standing beside my mother, trying to get a glimpse of the bloodied hand I was trying to hide.

"What happened to your hand?" Abigail asked, obviously concerned.

"I had an accident while I was sewing."

She looked confused. "But you're an excellent seamstress. You've never had an accident."

My mother turned and looked at Abigail. "Go to the bathroom and bring me some bandages from under the sink."

While Abigail was gone, my mother quickly retrieved bottles of rubbing alcohol and iodine from the kitchen cabinet. Holding my hand over the sink, she poured the clear liquid over my throbbing flesh. I took in deep breaths and, while concentrating, released the air in slow, measured increments. It was how we had been taught to bear pain. While my mother held a cotton ball over my hand, I wondered why I was trying so hard to protect Abigail.

Since reaching the age of accountability, she had already been exposed to the treachery inflicted upon members of the Community for even the smallest acts of disobedience. But in recent months, discipline had seemed to be increasing in frequency and severity, and shielding my little sister from it all had become almost instinctive.

"What were you doing to get into trouble this time?" my mother snapped. She lifted the cotton ball, poured water on the wound, and then reapplied pressure.

"I was listening to the men's conversation in the next room while sewing in the kitchen."

She let out a heavy sigh, and I knew she thought as much as I did that it was a ridiculous thing to be punished for. Before she could say anything about it, Abigail returned to the kitchen. She held out a bandage that was too small to hold back the steady flow of blood that was streaming from the wound.

My mother was not a person who was always able to stay calm, but for Abigail's sake, she seemed to be temporarily managing. "Thank you, dear. Now I want you to check over your homework before dinner."

"I've already checked it. I'm sure the answers are all correct."

"Check them again. I'll call you when I need you to help me in the kitchen."

Abigail dutifully went to her room while my mother soaked my hand in iodine again before bandaging the wound with a clean dishcloth. The next morning, she cleaned it and changed the bloody cloth, covering it this time with a large bandage. My hand was partially numb, and I had difficulty moving my fingers for several days.

Elizabeth McVeigh knew how to train her girls. I never looked away from my work again after that.

## Counselor

I've started shaking again. The counselor has her arms around me, and I'm certain she's keeping my emotions from spilling out and filling all the spaces around us.

"That's enough for today," she says, not letting go until my breathing returns to normal.

"But I'm remembering more."

She leans back and looks at me, trying to decide if she should let me go on.

"Please, just a little longer."

She's surprised that I'm the one who wants to keep going. Usually, she has to prod me and dig through my subconscious like she's mining through hard rock. But the fragments of memory are pouring out like waves of icy water, waking my subconscious. I'm afraid if I don't open the floodgates and let everything out, I'll drown in the memories.

She sits back and looks at me, still trying to decide if we should continue. Perhaps she sees it in my eyes, the need to let it all out. She nods slowly. "Okay, a little bit longer."

I remember the first time we ventured toward the north meadow after the fire that wasn't supposed to be there… the fire that birthed the Burning Tree. I organize my thoughts and then tell her how the Burning Tree came to be.

"A few days after the fire had been put out, Alison, Lynette, Katie, and I were taking our time gathering wood and stretching out the precious moments we were allowed to be together without adult supervision. We began wandering toward the meadow, each step taking us closer to the tree. It was almost instinctive, as if something were drawing us there."

I'm calm now, thinking about our time together. Even a short distance from the Community, I seemed to feel a sense of relief. I relished the days when the elders set out four wheelbarrows instead of two by the wood storage container. It meant we were to bring back twice as much wood, and we would be allowed up to an hour together to complete the task.

I close my eyes, and in the theater of my mind, I see my friends standing against the backdrop of the rising moon, the lustrous branches of the beautiful cottonwood tree glowing in the light.

"What happened during that time?" the counselor asks.

"Everything in the field burned. The winter saplings, the twigs, the brush, every last bit of grass, and all the stems of the withered wildflowers… except for one tree."

I grab hold of the sides of the chair I'm sitting in before I speak again. This time, my eyes are wide open, and the tree, in all its glory, stands right before me.

"It was a large, beautiful cottonwood, the long, bent branches perfectly shaped. Of course, it was winter, and there were no leaves on the tree, but the bark had a spectacular sheen from the trunk, extending up through the branches."

I looked away from the tree and back at the counselor. When I saw a slight smile, I almost smiled myself. Then I saw the flames rising along the trunk and extending to the ends of the branches, and still, the bark was never consumed.

"Of course, this miraculous tree in all its mystery and splendor was not lost on the elders," I say softly. "After that first fire, it was all they could talk about."

"And what did they say about it?" She leans back in her chair and seems genuinely interested in what the answer to that question would be.

"They called it the *Burning Tree*," I say softly, staring past the sofa, the desk, and the decorative wall hangings in the office, straight into the north field and the magnificent cottonwood. "They insisted the tree's amazing survival was a sign from God, a sign that everything wicked, impure, and unnatural should be destroyed. And that somehow, we would cleanse ourselves through the power of that tree."

# Chapter Five

I t's Tuesday evening, and fire and brimstone are falling on the Community like January hail. Hayden McVeigh is in rare form. I've heard many fiery sermons before, but nothing like this. His face contorts into a shape that makes him nearly unrecognizable, but his words are as crisp and clear as a morning sky.

"And we know witches are living just beyond the north meadow!" He pounds his fist on the podium, and I feel the vibration under my feet. But it's the sound of his voice that captivates me. It rings in my ears like the growl of an angry cougar searching for prey in the Laramie Mountains. Even Alison is paying attention.

"We can see their fires burning in the distance, as bright as the moon. Fire creeping up from hell itself is closing in on us!"

He looks as if he's actually experiencing the heat from the fire. The sweat pools in tiny beads across his forehead, dripping along the sides of his freshly shaven face. When he stopped to breathe, turned a page from his notes, or even shifted his weight against the podium, someone in the front row would jump. As we sat shoulder to shoulder, I could feel the fear rippling down the row from one human body to the next.

"The cottonwood tree in the north field is proof!" he bellowed over the deafening silence. "The tree is holy, and the witches have no power over it! The tree is strong and powerful. Its branches stretching toward the heavens represent obedience, even in nature."

While he preached, Elder McVeigh would lock eyes with those of us in the front row, one by one. He did it almost continuously, left to right, and then back again. When he looked down at me, I could feel the heat from his eyes. I was certain that at any moment my entire body would catch on fire, and I'd burn to death right there in the front row.

"Our young people in the Community, coming of age in such perilous times, will be tested beyond what they are possibly able to endure. They must be strong, like the cottonwood tree. They must be obedient even in the face of evil, death, and hellfire, just as the tree that was engulfed in flames but refused to burn!"

I could hear the light sound of someone digging their shoe into the soft wooden floor. I opened and shut my eyes several times, hoping each time I opened them that Hayden McVeigh would disappear.

"Being obedient means those in the Preparation must focus intently on their work for the Community, giving 100 percent to the Preparation and everything it represents. They must submit to the authority of the elders and those who will become their future elders."

I breathed deeply and slowly while the faces of our elders, and those who would be our future elders, presented themselves in the theater of my mind. Hayden McVeigh, Jonathon Alden, and Timothy Lane. Then I pictured Robbie and Patrick McVeigh, the future elders of the Community. Submission to these men seemed strange, and I felt an unnamed fear growing in the pit of my stomach at the thought of submitting to their every demand.

For several minutes, he talked about the Preparation and the role each of the young people coming into adulthood would play. The boys began to perk up when he talked about hunting, breeding animals, and the many jobs that young men would train for during the Preparation. Then he talked about marriage and starting a family, and some of the activities the girls would participate in.

But this respite was short-lived, and Elder McVeigh soon returned to the witches and the Burning Tree, as he so often did now. He stiffened his back, drew a breath, and seemed to meditate upon that thread of oxygen. When he released it, it came bursting out with warning, admonition, and a plan of attack.

"Sin must be destroyed, completely! Or else it will grow like a venomous weed and choke the life right out of us! The evil that has come near us in the form of the witches cannot be allowed to infiltrate our Community. The Scripture is clear! Exodus 22, verse 18 states – 'Thou shalt not suffer a witch to live!'"

I was sitting so close to Katie that her right arm and leg were practically on top of me. Thankfully, she was small and I could easily bear the weight. I could feel the goosebumps on her arms. "What was the verse?" she whispered, barely audible into my ear.

Sometimes the elders would question us the following day regarding the sermon. Not knowing could result in a minor punishment. One of the Bader boys had been forced to run a mile barefoot through the north meadow after staring out the window too long during one of Jonathan Alden's sermons. Melissa Smyth's older brother had been denied food for 24 hours after not being able to answer questions about one of Hayden McVeigh's sermons.

I swallowed, took a deep breath, and mouthed the words, "Thou shalt not suffer a witch to live, Exodus 22:18."

Katie's head nodded in slow motion.

I had been trying to listen as attentively as possible for the last fifteen minutes. When I could no longer force myself to concentrate, I looked slightly to my right, searching for a diversion. The angry, sulking face of Elizabeth McVeigh provided, if not a better diversion, at least a different one.

Elizabeth McVeigh had a face that looked like it had been washed with a scouring pad. She had red, sun-chapped cheeks and hard lines around her mouth and forehead, brought on by years of working outside and constant frowning.

She was the one who had caught me listening to the forbidden iPod and had proceeded to drag me like a rag doll to confess in front of her husband and the other elders. It was Elizabeth who had slammed my hand into a large sewing needle. Even though I'd never been told it was so, I knew it was wrong to hate another human being. But I did. I hated Elizabeth McVeigh.

Finally, I heard the words, "Let us pray."

My prayers were not so much talking to God as trying to find Him. I'd plead, beg, ask Him where He was, and why I was here. But today, I only had the strength to close my eyes, overwhelmed by Elder McVeigh, standing in the pulpit only a few feet away from me.

***

We were released from the sanctuary and told to go directly to our place in the Preparation. Katie would be sent to Elizabeth McVeigh's home to continue her training as a seamstress. Alison had been given an unconventional job for a girl – skinning and tanning hides. It was something she claimed to enjoy immensely, and I was not surprised at all when it was decided she would be trained as a tanner in the Community.

Lynette was in training to become a midwife. Because her grandmother was the Community herbalist and a highly respected elderly woman, Lynette had been given the opportunity to prove herself in what was a coveted position.

With Hayden McVeigh's sermon still echoing in my brain, I sloshed through the snow to the greenhouse with a renewed sense of purpose and determination. I would be obedient and vigorous in the duties I was called to perform. My part in the Preparation was one that I loved, and I reasoned it would be easy to remain obedient and keep the witches from causing me to sin.

My place in the Community was not as important as the position of a midwife or an herbalist, but more important than a cook, a seamstress, or many other positions a woman could have. I was on equal footing with the hunters and fishermen in the Community, all of whom were men. That would put me in a good position for marriage, my mother had told me. One's skill in the Community was almost as highly regarded as a person's physical condition.

My role as a gardener and greenhouse caretaker had been determined when Jonathon and Kathleen Alden saw the success of my mother's backyard garden. As one of the primary cooks in the Community, she had been permitted to grow a rather large garden.

They had surveyed the garden last summer when the green beans were as thick as a man's finger. There had been succulent, bright red tomatoes as big as baseballs drooping on the vines. Onions and cabbages covered the ground, mature and ripe. I had hoped to be chosen as the next gardener, and my mother's bountiful crop had secured the position for me.

I would be the sole caretaker for the plants and vegetables we grew during the cold months in the greenhouse. Then I would transplant as many as possible and help tend to the Community gardens in the summer months.

Besides spending time with Abigail, I was probably happiest when in the greenhouse. I was almost always alone when I was there and completely surrounded by the tranquility and beauty of dozens of plants and flowers. Gretchen Lane, a pretty, young wife of one of the elders, was teaching me the art of horticulture.

It was a balmy 55 degrees when I entered the greenhouse. I hung up my coat and scarf as soon as I shut the door behind me and immediately began my regular routine. Within minutes, I noticed the greenhouse was not how I'd left it the day before. I was certain there were several items out of place. I knew the greenhouse inside and out, and objects as seemingly insignificant as a watering can or a bowl of seeds left on a table had to be in their exact place, or else I would instantly know.

My heart was racing almost as quickly as the random thoughts in my mind. Perhaps Elder McVeigh was right, and witches were living near our Community. He told us in sermons how tricky and conniving they could be. He said they could play tricks with a person's head, even make someone go crazy.

I picked up the watering can lying on its side and gently placed it back on the ledge. I carefully rearranged the soil around the radish plants that were plucked out far too early. I cleaned up everything that was out of place, trying to come up with a plausible explanation for why I'd found the greenhouse such a mess.

The kids in the Community  that was the answer. The 11 to 14-year-olds were not always supervised. They must have run in here during one of their games. Perhaps they were playing tag or hide-and-seek and knocked over a few items. I breathed a sigh of relief, finally coming up with something that could have happened, whether it did or not.

I didn't have time to second-guess myself. Gretchen came in only moments later. "We have so much work to get done today," she said quickly. "We need to start the tomato seeds, ground a new batch of fertilizer, and move the flowers to the east wall."

I nodded, eager to begin working. She surprised me when she said that we would start making the fertilizer. She reached above both our heads for the metal bucket that sat on the upper shelf.

Her tiny body looked funny as she stretched out her long, thin arms and stood on the tips of her toes. She was a long, fluid line except for the firm, round ball that was now her pregnant stomach.

We quickly arranged all the ingredients for the fertilizer on a wooden table that was set against the north side of the green-house. There were old coffee grounds, dried grass clippings, and eggshells. The coffee was mixed with grass clippings and manure from the chicken house. Eggshells were rinsed and crushed for the flowers. While I worked the eggshells, Gretchen took a hand spade and vigorously began mixing the coffee, grass, and ma-nure.

We both worked without conversation for several minutes. During that short time, I'd become proficient at scooping up the eggshells, crushing them into a fine mix of dust, and then adding small amounts of soil. The bandage on my hand hadn't been changed in several days and was loose along the top.

When a few crushed eggshells found their way between the dirty cloth and my swollen hand, it stung nearly as badly as when Elizabeth McVeigh had smashed the needle into my hand.

I tried not to scream, but I couldn't help myself when the jagged eggshells dug into the tender portion of my palm. Gretchen didn't seem alarmed by my sudden scream. She did, however, stop what she was doing.

"Let me see your hand," she said. Everyone in the Community knew what had happened. Any punishment or discipline was always public knowledge to keep others from stepping out of line.

"I'll wash it off and then rewrap it tighter. I'm sure this is painful," she said while pouring a cup of water over the palm of my hand. "But it's a pinprick. There won't be much of a scar after it heals."

She wrapped the bandage tightly around my hand, waiting for me to respond with something such as... *Oh, you're right... I'm so thankful... I only got my hand smashed with a needle... and the only scar left will be on my soul, so no one will ever see it.*

I couldn't bring myself to say those words out loud, but she could see the indignation in my eyes and proceeded to enlighten me regarding how thankful I should be.

As soon as she'd finished with my bandage, she began unbuttoning her blouse. I was so startled that I couldn't do anything but watch her release each button until she had enough undone to slip the blouse down halfway and pull out her left arm.

I gasped at the sight of several long, thin scars between her shoulder and elbow.

"I have five on my left arm and three on my right," she said. "I was horribly weak in the beginning. But I learned to bear the pain more quickly than most of the others. That was one of the reasons I was given in marriage to a man of high standing in the Community."

"How did it happen?" I asked softly.

She looked away from me, staring at the flowers along the east wall of the greenhouse.

"Razor blades."

I tried to act like the thought of razor blades slicing through a young girl's arm in an attempt to make her strong didn't bother me as much as it did.

"I won't go into the details," she said stiffly. "They're not important now anyway. Just know, there are worse things than what has happened to you."

She pulled her blouse back over her shoulder and quickly buttoned and tucked her shirt neatly into her skirt. Without a word, we returned to our work as if we'd never taken off on this strange diversion of Community discipline and learning to bear pain.

I found it difficult to mentally shift gears again and concentrate on my work. I took slow, deep breaths, counting in my head as I released the air.

She commented on how well the garlic was growing, that the lettuce was at least a week ahead of schedule, and that the tiny cabbage plants needed just a little more water. I knew the cabbage didn't need a bit of water, but I didn't argue. She smiled contentedly when we passed by the beets, the broccoli, and the flowering cauliflower.

When we came to the radishes, I feared she would notice that the soil had recently been replanted. But the baby must have kicked at that moment. She touched her stomach and looked down as we passed the radish plants.

Gretchen left a short time after that, leaving me to relish the remaining hour I had in the greenhouse before it would be time to meet the other girls for chores. I usually had my most pleasant thoughts of God during this time of the day.

Perhaps this God, who so often frightened me and whose judgment I continually feared, had an entirely different side to him that the elders hadn't told us about. After all, this God I hoped for had given us the beautiful fireweed flower that grew six feet tall in the heat of the summer, the wild iris in the most stunning shades of lavender imaginable, and the glacier lily with amazing curled petals as bright as the sun.

As soon as I left the greenhouse and stepped back into the Community, God seemed to drift back into the clouds, hidden somewhere among the mountains. And my understanding of Him shifted back, not to what I had briefly experienced, but to what I had been told for as long as I could remember.

The other girls had already gone to collect their rations of wood and kindling for the day. I knew how slowly they worked and how long they took to gather wood so they could stay away from the Community as long as possible. We weren't to wait on anyone who was late for a chore, but I figured I could catch up before they finished.

Tilting my head back, I breathed in the thin, crisp air. It felt good moving in and out of my lungs. The birds flying overhead were unhindered and unafraid. Their wings seemed to slide through the frozen air like silk feathers on sheets of unbroken ice.

I was not paying attention to my surroundings when I felt a hand on my shoulder. I started to scream, but the hand covered my mouth before the sound could escape. I turned around and saw those eyes, always those icy gray eyes when he got too close. And then I couldn't scream, even when he removed his hand. His eyes were like small pendulums a hypnotist would use to lull his patient into submission.

Patrick smiled. "And where are we going this lovely evening?"

"Chores. I need to gather wood." I desperately tried to sound strong and in control.

He let his hand drop to my shoulder before it grazed the length of my back.

"I guess you missed the others. You could come and help me. I'll tell the elders you were with me. I guarantee you won't get into any trouble."

Even though I didn't know what he wanted help with, I knew in general terms that it meant I could go places and do things that were not available or allowed for the average citizen in the Community. And for a brief moment, I was tempted.

Not having to haul wood sounded good. But then I looked into those eyes again, as cold and vast as an empty sky.

"I have to get going. The others will be mad if I don't do my fair share." He couldn't argue with that, so he came up with something else.

"I need help at the cabins later tonight. I'm doing some work out there."

The cabins weren't any place special to go. I could have gone there myself, even though I wasn't supposed to.

"I need to get going," I said, barely above a whisper.

He reached up and touched my ponytail, and I froze. With a quick tug, my hair instantly tumbled onto my shoulders. I instinctively reached for the rubber band, but he held it over his head as if he were playing a childish game of keep-away.

I tried in vain to pull it out of his hands. Each time I was close to grabbing it, he raised his hand higher. But his free hand managed to drape down the front of my body in the process. Katie was right about Patrick. And now his inappropriate behavior was spilling over me like poison.

Suddenly, that voice came from out of nowhere, breaking the air between us like thunder. "Patrick, you need to come help me. We have to get those guns cleaned so we'll be ready first thing tomorrow morning."

I spun around to see Hayden McVeigh standing in the road behind us. I know I trembled enough that Patrick had probably felt my fear. He smiled and said, "Sure, I'll be right there."

Hayden McVeigh nodded in the direction of his younger brother and then turned his steely gaze toward me. "You better get to your chores before you find yourself in trouble."

I was expected to say, "Yes, sir," but I didn't. I was so angry I couldn't bring myself to do anything but grab the rubber band out of Patrick's cold hands. I started running and didn't stop until I was in the thickest part of the woods.

# CHAPTER SIX

"**Y**ou're right about Patrick," I said without hesitation.

Katie slowed down and looked straight at me while we both continued walking. "So you thought I was making it all up?"

It sounded strange to hear anger in Katie's voice. Katie never got mad at anyone.

"No, I always believed you. I guess things seem more real when you experience them yourself."

"I don't know about Lynette or Alison," Katie said. "But that makes three of us, he feels the need to do such horrible things to."

"Three of us?" I asked.

"Both he and Robbie won't leave Whitney alone either."

I hadn't known about Whitney, but it didn't surprise me. She was so pretty. All the boys just naturally were drawn to her.

Suddenly, Katie grabbed my arm, tighter than I thought she was capable of, and we stopped in the middle of the main road. "Under or over?" she whispered.

We were almost to Kathleen Alden's home when she asked that question. "What do you mean, under or over?"

She leaned toward me and whispered. "Over the clothes or under the clothes? Lynette and I came up with that term, so in case anyone would hear us, they wouldn't know what we were talking about."

I could hardly believe what I was hearing. I whispered the word, over, just as Kathleen Alden opened her front door. "Come in, girls. You're right on time."

I couldn't help but wonder if it had been over or under for Katie. As frightened as she'd been recently, I didn't need to ask her. I already knew the answer. But I didn't want to think about it for a second longer. Kathleen Alden's pretty house with elegant furnishings and the sweet aroma of scented candles was a distraction I desperately needed.

As proper young ladies in the Community, we were expected to flip on happiness and congeniality like a light switch. When events such as weddings, birthday parties, or weekend dinners and dances took place, we were supposed to paint on our happy faces and express our joy at being young ladies coming of age in the Community.

Tonight was one of those occasions. Everyone would gather for dinner and dancing, and for girls in the Preparation, almost as much time was put into getting ready as the actual event.

Eleven girls were going through the Preparation, and we each arrived at Kathleen Alden's home two hours before dinner would be served at the Community Hall. We would be painstakingly prepared to look our best for potential suitors so that before the end of the year, we would be paired off in marriage.

Chairs were meticulously arranged throughout the kitchen and in the living room. Beside each chair were little tables filled with brushes, pins, curlers, makeup, and other beauty supplies. There were tubes of ruby red lipstick, extra lush mascara, velvety eyeliner, and cases full of glossy eyeshadow.

Supposedly, these items were all brought to the Community when the ladies had first moved here. But that had been several years ago for most of them, and some of the cosmetics cases weren't even open and still had plastic wrapping.

I picked up one of the eyeshadow cases on the table by my chair. It shone under the dull glare of the kerosene lamp. I was mesmerized by the pearly, rich colors.

"Okay, girls, we'll start the evening with a word of prayer," Kathleen Alden announced. "Then we'll pair you off with a married lady so you can get ready for the dinner."

The prayer was quick and to the point. "Bless our time together. May we stay obedient to the elders and the ways of the Community, amen."

And then our time to be made beautiful for the young men in the Community began. We all sat as still as statues while being fussed over by middle-aged women who were considered long past their prime.

After our make-up and hair were completed and we had each been given a dress to wear for the evening, Elizabeth McVeigh pointed toward the second bedroom and ordered us to undress. The master bedroom would have provided much more room, but the eleven of us were sent to the bedroom occupied by Kathleen's two young daughters. The girls, eight and eleven, thankfully weren't at home.

It made me uneasy that the curtains were not completely closed, but we had been warned repeatedly not to touch anything unless specifically given permission whenever we were in an elder's home. We crowded in, shoulder to shoulder, each of us instinctively trying to find a spot as far away as possible from the partially drawn curtains.

I tried to forget that I was getting undressed in a strange house, surrounded by several other girls, most of whom I barely knew. I hated being undressed down to my underwear in front of the competition.

Everyone's eyes were staring and exploring while pretending not to look at each other. I couldn't care less what the rest of the girls looked like underneath their T-shirts and overalls, so I concentrated on the pretty pink bedroom Kathleen had painstakingly decorated for her two daughters.

The bunk beds were intricately carved and covered with gorgeous, thick quilts. The closet doors weren't completely closed, and I could see dolls, stuffed animals, and other toys packed tightly inside.

Being embarrassed about slipping off my white T-shirt melted under the anger of realizing the elders' children enjoyed a designer bedroom while Abigail and I spent each night sleeping on a stubby pine bed over a cold wood floor. I should have just stared at their naked bodies instead of letting myself get so worked up about it.

I had just pulled down my overalls when Lynette made the strangest sound I'd ever heard. It was like a yelp, and then she covered her mouth with both hands before it could turn into a full-blown scream.

"What is it?" Alison demanded, more annoyed by the interruption than concerned by whatever had happened to Lynette.

"There's a face... in the window!"

We all covered ourselves as quickly as possible while turning our heads toward the window. Alison, in bra and underwear, stomped across the room and peered out into the oncoming darkness that lay just beyond the bedroom window.

The sun had set, and the last glimmers of twilight were fading into the Laramie Mountains. "I don't see anything. You probably saw an animal," Alison said.

"It didn't look like an animal," Lynette said, just above a whisper. "It was a head with a pale face and unruly hair."

*A pale face... unruly hair...*

I stepped into my dress as quickly as I could. The straps on my bra were too long and kept falling off my shoulders. But I wasn't going to take the time to adjust them now.

As soon as the dress was pulled over my shoulders, I immediately disliked it. It was pink and full of ruffles and bows. It belonged more on an ornamental doll propped up on a shelf than on a sixteen-year-old. Even Abigail had outgrown a dress like this.

Then Whitney screamed. "There is someone out there! I saw him!" She ran over and closed the curtains. She was still holding the curtains shut, the material clenched in her tiny hand, when Elizabeth and Kathleen rushed into the bedroom.

"A man's face is looking at us through the window," Lynette said. "I think..."

She stopped herself before she could say it was the face of Patrick that she saw. But we all knew that's exactly what she was going to say. Elizabeth must have known it as well; otherwise she wouldn't have been so angry.

"There's not a man's face looking through the window," Elizabeth insisted. "It's your evil mind playing tricks on you. You're lusting after a man, so you imagined seeing one when you got undressed."

I wanted to say, aren't we supposed to want a man? Isn't that what good Community women do, keep a man happy? Isn't that why we came here two hours before dinner, to be painted up like girls in a beauty pageant so we could attract a future husband? But no one dared say what each of us was thinking, not even Alison.

Kathleen softened the blow, taking some of the blame off of us. "Maybe it was the witches," she said firmly.

Elizabeth plodded over to the window and opened the curtains as wide as possible. Even though we were in Kathleen's house, Elizabeth outranked her as an elder's wife, and she had the power to take free rein in another woman's home. She stuck her face so close to the window that the tip of her nose touched the glass. "If there was anything out there, it's gone now," she insisted. "Finish getting dressed or we'll be late for dinner."

***

The fourth Saturday of every month, from approximately six in the evening until long after the moon had risen, the Community was transformed into a world that almost made sense. After the brutality of the competitions was over and long before we had to get up and scrub floors, sew dishcloths, and dodge punishments like they were poisonous darts, we could actually engage in activities that were enjoyable.

Tonight, the venison had been slow-roasted for hours and prepared in a thick glaze sauce that melted in my mouth. There were garlic mashed potatoes, green beans cooked in bacon, and desserts I was certain had been bought from a gourmet grocery all the way in Cheyenne. Without electricity or electronic devices, music was played on guitars, violins, and an old drum set that had been part of the band ensemble for as long as I could remember.

In those few sweet minutes that we ate, talked, and then lined up against the walls of the Community Hall, I could honestly say that I was happy. At least what I had known of happiness since coming to the Community.

As quickly as those moments of enjoyment had come upon me, they dissipated when the elders summoned us to the dance floor. We took our places in the middle of the Community Hall and waited for the boys to be called.

The elders watched with X-ray vision to see who the boys would choose to dance with. Whitney was always one of the first to be chosen. She was so pretty that the boys naturally flocked to her. One by one, the rest of us would be asked to dance. There was always an equal number of girls and boys each year in the Preparation, so matching up would never be a problem.

Once we had been paired together and the music started, they would watch the hands of awkward teenage boys sliding down the small of our backs. They would notice cheeks that seemed to rub dangerously close to an actual kiss. The elders watched us as we danced, their eyes focused on every move we made.

They were supposed to study our traits and characteristics, trying to see who made good matches and which young couples were awkward together. We were told repeatedly that this intense scrutiny was all done for the sake of marital matchmaking and eventual procreation.

The moment the older men cut in to dance with us – the men who had no business dancing with us because they were either too old or had wives of their own – the elders suddenly looked away as if we no longer existed.

"They're supposed to teach us how to dance and show us how to act around the boys," Katie said when we were waiting between songs to be chosen again. "That's why they cut in and dance with us. That's what my mother told me."

"Then why aren't their wives dancing with the younger guys? Why aren't they teaching them how to dance and how to act?" Lynette asked.

No one had an answer to that question, and I was thankful when the music started again and the awkward silence was drowned out by twangy banjos and guitars in desperate need of tuning.

Again, we were summoned to the dance floor. This time, Abner Coleman awkwardly grabbed my hand and pulled me into an embrace. He was too skinny, had a serious acne condition, and his hands were always cold. But I was still thankful to be dancing with him and not one of the older, married men.

"You're a pretty good dancer," he said nervously.

"Yeah, I'm not too bad – as long as I don't have to move around too much."

I didn't mean it to be funny, but he laughed anyway. It was an awkward laugh, but it made me feel safe and comfortable. I liked Abner and thought he was a nice guy. The thought of marrying him, however, made me nauseous, and so I purposely made an effort not to appear too interested.

Back and forth it went for what seemed like hours. We were almost constantly dancing. While the teenage boys and the older men took turns with us, the married women washed the dinner dishes and glared at us from behind tubs of dirty water.

Somehow, I had managed to avoid Patrick during several ro-tations. Eventually, my luck ran out, and I found myself pressed against his body, the ripples in his chest as hard as rock. Patrick was so strong. He was able to pull me next to him in such a forceful manner that I couldn't even attempt to resist.

Then he put his cheek next to mine. A chill ran down the length of my back. But that was nothing compared to his clumsy hands, both so large and powerful that they seemed to move without him.

I looked around, but no one was watching us except his wife. She looked at me with such hatred that for a second, I was more frightened of Celia than Patrick. Why in the world would she hate me and not him?

Patrick's young wife, Celia, was infertile and had struggled for years without success to provide even a single child for her husband. She had been visiting Ruth Anne Weber for years, dutifully taking herbs and following various natural techniques in her attempt to conceive. The Community midwives had come up with everything from standing on her head after sex to eating fried dandelion roots, but nothing had worked.

There were over a hundred people in the Community Hall, but I was all alone. I was alone, trapped in the arms of Patrick McVeigh and the angry eyes of his wife, Celia.

"Dance with me the way you danced with Abner," he said. It was more like a command than a request.

"You have a wife to dance with. Why do you even want to dance with me?"

He didn't say a word, but his smile was so wicked that my stomach instantly tied up in knots. I was certain I would throw up my dinner right there on the dance floor if he held me next to him for another second.

And then, miraculously, the music stopped. I pulled away from Patrick and practically ran to the chairs along the wall, gladly obeying the elder's instructions to return to the sidelines each time the music stopped.

It was announced that one of the strings on the guitar had broken, and we were given a short respite until it was fixed. I looked at Katie, who had been dancing with an old widower everyone knew was desperate to marry a young girl. She looked at Lynette, who had been dancing with Robbie. And then we all looked to Alison as if she were the only one with the strength or the intelligence to figure out what to do.

Alison suddenly said, "Let's all go out for some air while they're fixing the guitar."

We were allowed to go outside, but only in groups, and only for a short amount of time. We followed Alison out the side doors and then behind the Community Hall. As soon as we were all outside and away from the elders and their wives and every other adult in the Community, Alison took charge.

We were only outside for a second or two before Alison grabbed my wrist and took off for the meadow. She turned back and called for the others. "Come on! Follow me!"

"What are you doing? We can't just leave," I said.

But she didn't answer. She kept running, holding my arm, making sure I wouldn't turn back even if I wanted to. The cold air felt good. Both my face and hands had been burning inside – my face from the weight of layers of makeup and my hands from being held far too tightly by Patrick McVeigh.

Alison and I stopped in the clearing after the first cluster of trees and waited. I wondered what we would say if later questioned by the elders or their wives about why we were away. I started running through the excuses in my head.

When Lynette and Katie caught up with us, Alison started running again. It wasn't long before I knew she was heading toward the cabins. We weren't quite there when she stopped again behind a cluster of thick bushes.

"I smell smoke," Alison said. She tilted her head back and slowly breathed in the cold night air.

Alison pulled her sleeves down over her hands for protection against the thorns when she parted the branches. The rest of us leaned in behind Alison, attempting to get a good view of what was happening approximately twenty yards away in the next clearing.

"Look," Lynette whispered.

There was a small fire burning right in front of the cabin. It looked like someone had tried to put it out by covering it with dirt, but it was still smoldering enough that smoke was rising steadily.

"There really are witches living in the cabin!" Katie shrieked.

The rest of us said "Shhh!" at the same time and made more noise than Katie had.

Alison leaned forward and quickly scanned the area. "It doesn't look like anyone is there now."

Lynette, the most superstitious of all of us, slowly looked around in every direction. "Maybe you can't even see witches."

I tried to act brave when I definitely wasn't. "Let's take a look and see who's there."

Both Katie and Lynette turned and looked at me like I was crazy. Alison smiled and said, "Yeah, I think we should."

Alison again took my hand, knowing I'd never take the first step on my own. She also knew that Katie and Lynette would have pulled back and not followed her toward the smoldering fire. Both Alison and I kicked dirt over the remaining flames until there was nothing left. Without a word, Alison turned toward the cabins.

"We really shouldn't be going inside. It's obvious someone has been here," I said.

"Exactly. And we need to find out who it was."

I secretly hoped that the door of the first cabin was locked, but it wasn't. The inside was illuminated by the light of a nearly full moon that shone through a large front window. After we were inside, Katie and Lynette followed us.

"No one is here," Alison said, disappointed.

"But someone was," Katie said.

There was uneaten food in a bowl that didn't look like it had been there for more than a few hours.

I leaned over and smelled what looked like some kind of meat. "It actually smells good."

Lynette wrinkled her nose. "Gross."

"Why would witches be cooking and eating?" Katie said.

Alison rolled her eyes. "Witches have to eat like anyone else."

Lynette slowly shook her head and began to back away toward the door. "The elders are right. There really are witches here."

"Don't be ridiculous," Alison said sternly. "Besides, if they're invisible like you said, why would they have to eat?"

"I didn't say they were invisible," Lynette insisted. "I said maybe we can't see them. Those are two different things."

"But someone has been here," Katie insisted again.

"Maybe they're not witches," I said. "Maybe just a couple of homeless people stayed here for a while."

Lynette made a strange face. "Homeless people? In the middle of the Wyoming wilderness?"

No one said anything for several seconds, and the silence scratched at my brain like a jagged claw. I looked down again at the food. "We need to get back. Everyone has noticed by now that we're gone."

# CHAPTER SEVEN

We had been gone less than twenty minutes, but back at the Community Hall, the gossip spread faster than an August wildfire in the foothills of the Laramie Mountains. Mouths were chattering that the whereabouts of four teenage girls were suddenly unknown, and imaginations were almost certainly running wild.

When we finally did return and were questioned by the elders, it was starting to get late, and we were all tired. I suppose the tiredness helped to quench our nervousness, and we answered their questions calmly and without raising any suspicion.

We told the elders that the heat inside the Community Hall had been overwhelming. That was true. We also said we had only taken a brief walk in the general area and had not gone far. That was not true.

No one had seen us leave or return from the cabins, so we received only a verbal scolding. And with the expectation of impending discipline eliminated, everyone returned to talking about who was dancing with whom and who would eventually be matched up in marriage.

But I couldn't focus on dancing or even the upcoming engagements that would be announced within a few months. I couldn't stop thinking about the possibility of women practicing the dark art of witchcraft living in the cabins. That, and the reason we had left the dance was to get away from the roving eyes and pawing hands of Patrick and Robbie McVeigh.

That night, I struggled to sleep. When I finally drifted off, strange dreams involving witches and the elders left me tossing and turning. In my dream, I vividly remembered creatures dancing around a fire, laughing and chanting. When they turned to face me, it wasn't the faces of the witches I saw, but the elders.

***

Jonathon Alden, with his square jaw clenched in determination and his sapphire eyes blazing, leaned into the podium with such force that it sometimes tilted back. The more intense his sermons, the more the podium wobbled, teetering precariously on its edge. Sometimes, I feared he would push it off the stand, crushing the worst of us sinners in the front row.

According to Jonathon, God was always angry, ready to pounce and destroy, even if you begged for mercy. But God was especially mad today because there were girls in the Community that the elders were certain were guilty of horrible things.

Since the elders didn't have any proof we had done anything wrong the night of the dance, and there had been four of us insisting we had only gone for a walk near the Community Hall, they hadn't punished us. I suppose this was Jonathon's way of punishing us, chastising us from the pulpit, without naming us individually.

"We have known for some time that the servants of Satan have been in our midst." Jonathon stared straight at me, those blue eyes as wild as a raging sea.

"Perhaps God allowed us to build our Community in their midst to test our faith. Or maybe such evil nearby will enable us to see it among ourselves."

He hadn't come right out and said the words, but I knew he was not only talking about us but also the witches that supposedly were living in the cabins – and that several of us in the Community were suspected of visiting them. I thought about how we had gone to the cabins, had seen the fire burning, and the food inside still warm.

I shuddered and looked away from the podium. I couldn't bear to look at him as he spoke. I was certain he'd see the guilt in my eyes.

"Each one of them will burn in hell for all eternity!" he proclaimed. "As well as those who consort with them!"

I looked to the left and then to the right, just out of the corner of my eye without turning my head. I didn't want anyone to know I was looking around, but I had to see if Katie, Alison, and the other girls were still here. The way he was pounding his fist, his words filling the air like tiny pellets of hail, I was certain I was the only one left in the room, and at any moment the floor would drop beneath me and I would slide into the flames of Hell.

According to Jonathon Alden, there was one chance for redemption. He picked up the large Bible that was always set on a small table behind where the elders stood. He placed it on the podium and firmly pressed the pages open. The elders didn't often read from the Bible, but when they did, we paid attention.

He took off his black suit jacket and laid it neatly over the stool behind him. He stood tall and straight, his muscles rippling beneath his perfectly pressed white dress shirt.

"First Corinthians, chapter 9, verse 24," he said with a voice louder than I had ever heard. He looked down at the words and began reading.

*Know ye not that they which run in a race run all, but one receiveth the prize? So run, that ye may obtain. And every man that striveth for the mastery is temperate in all things. Now they do it to obtain a corruptible crown; but we an incorruptible. I therefore so run, not as uncertainly; so fight I, not as one that beateth the air: But I keep under my body, and bring it into subjection: lest that by any means, when I have preached to others, I myself should be a castaway.*

1 Corinthians 9:24-27

"The physical exertion we demand of our young people is to make them strong in both body and soul. And we don't require anything of you that we haven't already done ourselves," he said with confidence. He stretched his taut arms across the podium, revealing his own physical strength.

"I strike my body and bring it into subjection!" he suddenly yelled. He pounded his chest with a clenched fist, and the entire front row jumped.

"You must discipline yourselves! You must endure pain! If you are not able to do this, you will not only be disqualified from your earthly prizes, but your heavenly ones as well!"

Jonathon's admonition to be disciplined and to endure seemed to go on forever. Every so often, Katie's fingers would move slightly and twist around the ends of my own. We held on to each other, keeping one another from sliding into the pit of everlasting agony.

***

Less than ten minutes after I'd been in the Community Hall listening to Jonathon Alden, I was in the greenhouse, a million miles away from condemnation and fear. I worked hard but steadily for the next several hours.

When it was time to start cleaning up, I looked around the greenhouse, satisfied with everything I'd accomplished. I was sweaty and tired. The hard work had cleansed my body and my mind, and I felt much better now than when I started.

There was still a lot of work left to do in the cleanup process. Mud as thick as my finger lined the inside of both buckets I'd used when taking care of the vegetables. There was a watering system hooked up inside the greenhouse, but the water pressure was weak compared to the hydraulic water pumps outside.

The greenhouse was now as neat and clean as an indoor garden could be. To avoid any excess mess, I decided to take the buckets to the water station next to the small barn.

A gentle breeze flowing through the Community engulfed my face as I closed the greenhouse door and walked outside. It was a soft, easy breeze that seemed to pick up sounds from a distance and deliver them to my ears.

Of course, as soon as I saw Patrick and Alison, I was straining, leaning my head at just the right angle so any of the words they spoke would have an easier path. An unmarried female was never supposed to be alone for an extended amount of time with a man in the Community.

I suspected an exception had been made since Alison was training to be a tanner and Patrick was an expert in the profession. I wondered how she could stand being around him, even for something official like training for the Preparation.

The well was deep, and the hand pump was stiff after a particularly cold night. I didn't bother to hurry as I leaned down and pushed and pulled the long wooden handle. My hand moved up and down slowly so I would have time to watch what they were doing. The first thing I noticed was that Alison's hair was out of the usual ponytail we wore and was hanging over her shoulders.

As soon as the first bucket was filled about halfway, I swished the water around inside and then dumped the dirty water on the ground near the pump. While I was filling the second bucket, I saw Patrick and Alison lift a large deer hide over a pair of ropes tied between two poles. The ropes were used as drying racks for the skins of animals.

After the deer hide was properly positioned, Alison walked behind it. When Patrick followed her, I could only see their legs below the knees. From the knees down, I couldn't tell them apart. The baggy denim jeans that Patrick wore and the denim overalls on Alison were the same color and width. Even their shoes were nearly identical and almost the same size since Alison had big feet for a girl.

I took my time filling the second container, using my hands to wipe out the insides, and then carefully rinsing. After being filled with soap, they had to be rinsed several times to make sure the soapy residue was completely gone.

I wanted to get as close to where they were standing as I could. When I saw an extension hose lying about twenty feet away, next to one of the sheds, I saw my chance to get closer. I quickly retrieved it and attached it to the nozzle on the water pump.

While rinsing, I pulled the hose as far as it would go, getting as close as possible to where Patrick and Alison were standing while still doing exactly what I was supposed to do. I could hear their muffled voices and then their laughter.

That's when I could no longer pretend to be rinsing the bucket. I stood perfectly still, desperately trying to hear what they were saying, the hose pulled taut in my left hand as I leaned toward the deerskin.

Suddenly, I was confused, not because I couldn't hear or see what was happening, but because it was now obvious that Alison didn't hate being around Patrick as much as she told the rest of us. The rest of us were more than annoyed with the man and did almost everything we could to stay away from him. And Katie was genuinely terrified of him. Yes, Alison had to work with him, and she was stronger than the other girls, but I could sense now that something was different about what was happening between them.

As desperately as I tried, I couldn't make out the words, but what I saw next took my breath away. Her legs suddenly wrapped around Patrick's legs. He must have been holding her. I couldn't see anything above their knees, so I couldn't be sure. Then her legs touched the ground, and almost instantly, she was leaning against him, standing on her toes.

I knew I shouldn't have left my work for even a second, but curiosity got the best of me. I dropped the bucket and the hose, the water trickling steadily onto the frozen ground. I walked carefully toward the deer hide.

Without making a sound, I peered around the corner, pulling the thick skin back with my fingers. When I saw them, now up against the side of the barn, I couldn't believe my eyes. I stood there for several seconds and stared.

When I finally came to my senses, I slowly pulled back, realizing they were so preoccupied with one another that they hadn't even noticed I was there.

Looking in every direction and knowing no one had seen me, I went back to the buckets and hose. I stood there for the longest time, watching dribbles of water swirl into the metal bucket. No matter how hard I tried, I couldn't get the picture of Alison and Patrick out of my mind. It was seared in my memory.

Alison had been kissing Patrick. She had been willingly, even passionately, kissing him. His hands were all over her, in places they should never have been. He hadn't chased her down or forced himself on her. She had chosen to wrap herself around Patrick – a married man.

I took several heavy breaths before I looked down again and noticed the water from the hose was not going into the bucket. I quickly rearranged the hose and then looked in every direction, making sure no one had witnessed my careless behavior.

Even though I was closer to Katie and Lynette, I still considered Alison a good friend. The fact that she not only hadn't told me about what was so obviously happening between her and Patrick was painful enough. But that she pretended not to want anything to do with him, like the rest of us, was more than I could take. I took my rage out on the metal bucket, which still wasn't completely clean. I kicked it, stomped it, and beat it against the side of the pump.

"Girl, what are you doing?"

I jerked around to see Timothy Lane, Gretchen's husband, staring at me as if I'd lost my mind. Maybe I had.

"I couldn't get all the stuck mud out of the bucket. I was trying to get it cleaned out."

It was an outright lie, but one he couldn't prove. He also had a handful of fish from the creek he needed to clean. So I grabbed the buckets and hurried back to the greenhouse.

When I went home, I found a note from my mother letting me know that she and Abigail were delivering food to a family who had a new baby. I spent the next hour sitting in the darkness, letting my mind wander to all kinds of crazy places.

# Chapter Eight

Heavy leather jackets, fluffy wool coats, and dozens of handmade quilts and blankets were arranged at the front on the left side of the Community store on wooden shelves. On the floor beneath the shelves were boots and shoes from size 14 to tiny baby-sized shoes.

At the very front, on the right side, were women's dresses, men's pants and shirts, and dozens of denim overalls for every child in the Community who had not yet passed through the Preparation.

In tiny drawers next to the shelves were underwear, bras, and toiletry items that were hidden and weren't proper for display on open shelves. About a year ago, a few of the ten and eleven-year-old boys took tampons, male underwear, and ladies' bras and tossed them out the front door of the store.

For some reason, ten and eleven-year-olds think things like that are hysterically funny. Of course, once they were caught, the elders paddled their bare bottoms outside... in the freezing weather... with wooden paddles dipped in ice water. After their bottoms were beaten raw and some of the skin torn off, they never thought throwing personal items out of the drawers was funny ever again.

There had never been another incident in the store until the day after I'd seen Alison kissing Patrick behind the deerskin. Whether what happened in the store had anything to do with Alison kissing Patrick, I didn't know at the time. But I'd been so overwhelmed by what I'd seen that thoughts of them kissing seemed to interfere with every other thought I had in my head at the time.

The back room of the general store included a storage area with a small kitchen. It also contained an old-fashioned potbelly stove. This was where Jada Brewer, Lynette's grandmother, boiled and brewed herbs for all the medicinal needs in the Community.

Jada, whose specialty was growing, harvesting, and cooking medicinal herbs, was also in charge of minding the store during the daytime hours when it was open. Of course, no one actually purchased anything with cash. The Community had done away with the need for money.

Jada would ration out supplies and record who had taken what and how much. The elders would examine the books every week to make sure there was neither greed nor fraud among the members.

When there was no one in the store getting supplies, which was most of the time, she was in the back room brewing her herbs or teaching young girls the art of cooking. Alison and Whitney's turn came on an overcast Tuesday afternoon.

Whitney had always said that she wanted my mother to teach her how to cook. It wasn't that she didn't like Lynette's grandmother, but that she didn't feel safe in the back room of the general store, where anyone could come in at any moment.

I wasn't there when it happened, but Whitney explained everything to me later in painful detail. Whitney would even say that she was certain what had happened was a set-up; that it had to be because Patrick and Robbie often worked in pairs.

While Alison and Whitney were peeling potatoes and carrots to add to a massive pot of venison, the bell on the front door of the store clanged. Jada quickly leaned over Whitney's shoulder and stuck a fork in the venison as the boiling water bubbled up along the sides of the pot.

She took in a deep breath, drawing in the thick steam. "It's not ready for the vegetables yet. Let me see who's up front and what they need. By the time I get back, it should be ready. Keep cutting. That's not nearly enough potatoes."

Jada Brewer walked slowly with a slight limp because of the arthritis in her left hip. She was slow but steady, and if she yelled from the next room she was coming, you could count on it, but not for a while.

As Jada peeled open the curtain and stepped into the general store, Whitney could see who had come inside. Patrick McVeigh. She said she quickly stepped back and was certain he hadn't seen her. Patrick ambled into the front of the store, staying as close to the front door as possible so Jada would come to where he was.

"Who's here?" Alison had asked before dropping carrots into a pan of water to soak.

"Patrick," Whitney had said without looking up.

Whitney took the small knife, as sharp as a razor blade, and continued to slice the thick, brown skins off the potatoes. She had a smooth, rhythmic motion that at first impressed Alison.

But with each slice, Whitney's motions became more frantic and eventually erratic. She was slicing faster and faster until the knife became a blur. When Alison looked over and saw that the potato Whitney was holding was stained red, she grabbed hold of her hands.

"Stop it! He's out there, not in here."

"I know. I can't help it." Whitney was taking deep breaths, her chest slowly heaving in and out.

Alison pulled Whitney by the wrists to the sink and rinsed the blood off her hands. Thankfully, there were only two superficial cuts on her fingers. "Rinse your hands off and then wrap the cuts in a small dishcloth. I'm going up front to see what Patrick wants."

Whitney said everything was a blur after that. The dishcloth wrapped in and out between her fingers, the boiling venison, the wind at the back door, it was all annoying and distracting. Even the sound of her own footsteps, back and forth across the rickety wooden floor, was irritating.

Once Alison was up front with Patrick and Jada, Whitney felt relieved. She said she remembered thinking that Patrick couldn't get to her, not past both of them. But that was the planned illusion, the ploy that had fooled them all.

Whitney again picked up the knife and began to peel and slice the potatoes. This time, the motions were slow and easy, even monotonous.

Then, without warning, everything changed. She recalled the exact moment, feeling as if time had stopped, the earth had shifted, and everything had suddenly changed irrevocably and horribly.

There was dead silence, not even a shadow on the wall, but even so, she knew he was there. It was almost like a premonition, a dark fear that rose from the pit of her stomach. That's when Robbie shut the back door.

Whitney froze. Her feet wouldn't move, and she couldn't open her mouth. Everything unfolded in slow motion as he walked toward her without saying a word, those hands hanging by his sides, as thick as clay.

"A good woman learns how to cook," he said, nodding in satisfaction.

Whitney hadn't yet looked at him. She was grasping the knife so tightly her hands were trembling.

As he stood behind her, his fingers slid along the sides of her body like tentacles. When he reached around her, picked up a fork, and stuck it into the venison, she thought perhaps he was only toying with her. Maybe he'd stuff his face full of food and then be on his way. But after one bite, both hands returned to places on her body where they didn't belong.

"Leave me alone. I'm not going to say it again."

"Good, because it won't matter if you do."

She still had the knife in her hand, holding it down between the side of her leg and the stove. Her hands were shaking, causing the knife to click-click-click, like snapping fingers against the side of the stove. But he was too busy to hear it.

She pulled, twisted, and even used her knees to fend him off. Nothing was working, and he was getting farther and farther along, pulling at her clothes, tugging underneath them.

"Alison! Jada! Help me!" Whitney screamed.

What she didn't know was that Jada had gone outside with Patrick as he tried on a winter coat. He told her he wanted to see how warm it kept him before taking it. She had hobbled outside after him, standing on the main road as he buttoned the coat and shoved his hands deep into the pockets.

Being almost as hard of hearing as she was arthritic in the bones, Jada didn't hear Whitney's screams from the outside. Alison, still on the inside of the store, however, did and immediately ran to the back room to see what had happened to Whitney.

What she came back to was a bloody mess. Between the knife and a flurry of fists, a terrible fight had erupted.

"Let her go, Robbie!"

By the time Jada was back inside, with the coat in hand that Patrick had suddenly decided he didn't want, she finally heard all the commotion coming from the back room.

"What in the world is going on!" she cried. Dropping the coat on the floor, she began the slow, painful journey from the front of the store to the back room. Her right leg moved quite easily and freely, but moving her left leg was like pulling the weight of a dead log.

It seemed to take forever for Jada to get to the back room. Of course, she was old and feeble and wouldn't have been able to do much of anything anyway. But she would have at least been a witness; a respected older lady in the Community. It would have made all the difference regarding what would unfold over the next several days.

Whitney had not let go of the paring knife throughout the entire ordeal – not once. She got one good stab into the groin, and Robbie howled like a wounded animal when he finally gave up and ran out the back door. But this was before Jada had pulled the curtain to the back room open.

"What in heaven's name has happened back here!" Jada's legs stopped moving. She stared into a room splattered with blood, thrown food, and terrified young girls heaving in exhaustion.

"Nothing to do with heaven happened back here," Alison assured her.

"What did happen? What did you girls do?"

Whitney was too shaken to realize the implications of what Jada Brewer had just said, but Alison understood completely. Jada had immediately implied that whatever had happened had been their fault and that they had most certainly brought it upon themselves. And, of course, she had seen nothing, hadn't even known that Robbie had been there.

Whitney decided to tell her anyway. She said she had to explain in horrifying detail and scream the words to get them out of her head. But the words felt strange in her mouth, and the moment she had released them, she knew she shouldn't have.

"Robbie McVeigh attacked me! He sexually attacked me!"

Jada tilted her head and looked at Whitney as if she were speaking another language.

"How dare you say such a vile and hateful thing about an elder's son. Clean this place up immediately. We're finished for this evening."

Jada quietly pulled the curtain shut behind her and returned to the front of the store to finish her work.

Alison took slow, deep breaths as she rinsed a washcloth in the sink and began the task of cleaning up the blood. There was blood on the floor, on the cabinet, and sizzling on the stove where the burner hadn't yet been turned off.

"What are we going to do?" Whitney asked. "He... touched me, beneath my clothes."

Alison told me how she took hold of Whitney's shoulders. They were so frail and thin that she was afraid they would crack and break in the palms of her hands.

"We're going to finish cleaning up, and then we're going to go home and get a good night's sleep."

Whitney was horrified at the thought of just pretending it never happened. "He can't get away with this! We have to tell someone!"

"He has, and we did. If Jada Brewer won't help, no one will," Alison insisted.

Jada was one of the kindest ladies in the Community. She was stern and hard-working, but usually sympathetic and understanding. But she was also in denial... and very afraid.

Alison got Whitney cleaned up, scoured the back room, and threw away every bit of food that had been cooking. Alison then walked Whitney to her house before returning home. It was unthinkable that this would all be over, and they were just to pretend that nothing had happened. What they didn't know at the time was that it was only just the beginning.


## Counselor


"After Robbie attacked Whitney and Alison, I knew things would never get better in the Community," I whisper.

The counselor's head is tilted. "What exactly do you mean?"

"Up until that incident, I always had hope that, despite what was happening with Patrick and Robbie, eventually, things would change. I'd convinced myself that life was difficult because we were going through the Preparation or because Robbie was still single or Celia hadn't had a baby. I truly believed that once I got older or married or something, life in the Community would be good."

I shake my head and take a deep breath. "But after that, after two girls who were only defending themselves still managed to get into so much trouble, I knew that something was very wrong in the Community that marriage, babies, and even growing up couldn't fix. That's when fear and depression crawled into my brain and wouldn't leave."

My voice is dry and scratchy. I reach for the glass of water on the table and take a long drink. I look out the window at the clouds hanging in the sky like thick, dark coils.

"There's a storm coming in," the counselor says softly.

I squeeze my eyes shut and then quickly open them. The words "storm coming" jar a forgotten memory. It was what my mother had said after what had happened to Whitney at the store but before the trial and the punishments and everything else that exploded around us. I could never hear the words "there's a storm coming" and not think of what happened next in the Community ever again.

# Chapter Nine

Less than twenty-four hours after Whitney had fought off Robbie McVeigh, the Community elders had been consulted, and an emergency meeting was called. However, conflicting stories about what happened at the general store had already spread rapidly throughout the Community.

Of course, Whitney had insisted that Robbie had not only attacked her but that the attack had been sexual. Alison said she had come into the middle of a vicious battle and had attempted to break up what she now only referred to as a fight between two people.

Between the time Robbie had arrived on Ruth Anne Weber's doorstep, bloodied and needing stitches, and the moment we all began descending upon the Community Hall, the story regarding what had happened had morphed and mutated into something neither Whitney nor Alison could hardly believe.

The latest version of the story included Alison, and in particular Whitney, physically attacking Robbie only because he had come into the store after a day of hunting, hungry, and wanting a bowl of venison.

"It's time to bring this meeting to order!"

Hayden McVeigh's voice wasn't just loud; it was powerful. It echoed like thunder during a heavy rainstorm. Over 100 adults and at least a dozen teenagers gathered throughout the Community Hall, all talking at once, their heads stuck together while their mouths moved like chattering wind-up toys.

Most of the adults had come inside in a disorderly manner, each wanting to know what had happened and what would be done about it. If there was anything Hayden McVeigh hated, it was disorder.

Hayden cleared his throat, and the entire room fell into silence. "Because of the brutality of this vicious attack, there will be a trial to determine the guilt or innocence of Whitney Crouse and Alison Flowers. And then, if necessary, the proper punishments will be determined. The trial will begin Thursday at 10 am."

Later that day, my mother would tell me that there had only been one other trial since we had come to the Community. It had taken place years earlier, not long after we had arrived, and I had no memory of it.

A woman named Rebecca had been accused of adultery and later found guilty. The elders reported that she had been attacked by a wild animal and killed during a wind cleansing. Her body was never found.

***

Thursday proved to be an unusually warm day as we all gathered in the Community Hall for the trial of Whitney Crouse and Alison Flowers. Ruth Anne Weber was to testify first, followed by Whitney, Alison, Jada, and finally, Robbie.

Upon hearing there would be a trial and she would have to testify, Jada Brewer fell ill and was being nursed by another elderly lady in the Community. Since she had not witnessed the attack and had not seen Robbie after what had happened, Hayden and Jonathon recused her from testifying.

I sat in one of the middle pews, my mother following close behind me. I was hoping to remain as inconspicuous as possible, blending into the middle of the crowd of Community onlookers.

I was glad Abigail wasn't here to witness the spectacle that was about to unfold. The elders, in a rare show of mercy, had decided that those in the Community who were fourteen and under were to remain in the care of several of the older women during the duration of the trial.

The elders didn't spend time on formalities, explanations, or introductions. As soon as everyone was quiet, they started the trial. Alison and Whitney were seated in the front row on the left side of the Hall, while Robbie and Ruth Anne were on the other side. Each of the elders was seated on the platform near the podium. Hayden McVeigh slowly rose to his feet, and the trial began.

# The Testimony of Ruth Anne Weber

"I call Ruth Anne Weber to the stand," Hayden McVeigh announced.

Ruth Anne was already standing before Hayden McVeigh had finished saying her name. The clickety-click of her stiff, black shoes on the wooden floor grated against my already frayed nerves. She straightened her skirt and freshly pressed blouse as she walked to the plain wooden chair that served as a witness stand.

Ruth Anne placed her hand on the massive Bible and swore to tell the whole and complete truth.

"Tell us, Mrs. Weber, exactly what happened the evening Robbie McVeigh came to your home looking for help."

Ruth Anne was portly, graying at the temples, and in general an unattractive woman. Her overall disposition wasn't much better. But she prided herself on her medical expertise and had an aura of arrogance that spilled out with every word she spoke. She adjusted her weight, and the chair next to the podium creaked under the strain.

"When Robbie showed up at our home, he looked absolutely terrible," she began. "Even though most of the wounds the girls had inflicted were superficial, each had bled considerably in the time it took to get to our front door. Blood was streaming down his face, matted in his hair, and soaked into his shirt."

I imagined Robbie putting on the performance of a lifetime while gasping for breath, rolling his eyes, and leaning against Ruth Anne's door as if he'd collapse at any moment.

"The poor young man had a stab wound in his groin area, not far from his private parts," Ruth Anne said, her face turning a bright shade of pink.

Hayden McVeigh spun around on his heels and glared at Whitney and Alison. "You were trying to emasculate my son! Cutting off a man's penis is the work of the witches!" he cried.

The Community Hall erupted into unbridled emotion, and this time, Hayden did nothing to stop the chaos. For what seemed like an incredibly long time, everyone talked and gasped and imagined this terrible deed of taking a knife and striking at the very heart of Robbie's manhood. As soon as there was a lull in all the commotion, Hayden McVeigh again questioned Ruth Anne.

Her eyes fluttered as she looked around the Community Hall. "I didn't see him when he first came to our door, only after my husband had helped him to the kitchen table. But he looked just plain awful. I could see more blood on him than skin and hair."

She stopped talking and looked down at her hands, the hands that had stitched up his wounds with a needle and thread.

Hayden walked up to the witness stand and made the saddest face I'd ever seen on another human being. "We know how painful this is. But try, if you can, to tell us what happened next."

"We wiped him up the best we could," she said, her voice softer. "I put salve on what I figured would heal quickly and stitched up the rest. I've never seen anything like this happen since I've been in the Community."

Up to that point, I suppose Ruth Anne told the whole truth, at least what she believed the truth to be. But then everything changed, and her testimony became strange, even frightening. I wasn't sure if she believed what she was saying or if the thoughts in Hayden McVeigh's head somehow found their way into Ruth Anne's mouth.

"I swear there was venom in that man's wounds," she said, raising her voice. "The witch's brew was seeping into his skin from where she attacked him."

A sudden murmuring of voices rose over the words "witches brew" and hung in the air like a dark cloud.

As soon as Ruth Anne left the witness chair, Hayden McVeigh turned abruptly and faced the congregation. "I call Whitney Crouse to the stand."

## The Testimony of Whitney Crouse

Whitney looked so small and frail sitting on the stand. Her beautiful blue dress and hand-sewn collar matched the cornflower in her eyes.

In those few seconds before the questioning began, I couldn't take my eyes off her. She reminded me of one of those lovely paintings hanging in the children's section of the library I used to visit as a little girl. She sat completely still. Her eyes were held wide open by the anticipation of what was about to happen.

The elders marched around the stand, their large bodies hovering over the top of her with dark eyes staring and large hands pointing gnarly fingers in her scared face. After talking among themselves, it was decided that Jonathon Alden would take over from here and question Whitney.

"After spending hours in the wilderness hunting to provide for our Community, Robbie McVeigh wanted nothing but a taste of the venison you were cooking. And you, in vicious anger, attacked him?"

"No, no, of course not." Her voice was weak and frail.

"Why would two young girls become so violent so quickly?" Jonathon Alden asked.

He turned toward the Community, more than happy to give them the answer to that question. "It is almost certain that witches have taken residence in the cabins beyond the north meadow. We've seen the smoke from the cabins and have found evidence that they have stayed there when we've gone to investigate. But with their dark powers, they can vanish as quickly as the smoke from the fires."

The Community Hall was completely quiet. Jonathon, a more eloquent speaker than even Hayden, had completely captivated and captured our attention quickly and effortlessly. Now that he had drawn us in and opened our minds, he was ready to fill in the empty spaces in our brains with the conclusion the elders had already come to.

"The spiritual influence their presence has had on such impressionable young girls is insidious. Their evil is overwhelming, but it is not excusable if someone has chosen of their own free will to revel in their presence."

He turned quickly and was instantly facing Whitney. Startled, she fell back into the chair. "Have you ever been to the cabins beyond the north meadow?"

I had to concentrate or I was afraid I'd stop breathing. I was certain that if I didn't think about it, the air would disappear. I knew lying was wrong. Being caught in a lie was a punishable offense, but I hoped with all my heart that she did lie, that she simply and quickly stated that she had never in her life been to the cabins.

But I knew Whitney well enough to know she would not lie. She believed that if she were as honest and forthright as possible, this would all be over quickly. There might have been a time when I believed that, too, but not now.

"Yes... we've been there."

At that moment, the room erupted with gasps of disbelief and a commotion among Community members that only Hayden McVeigh rising to his feet could silence. I leaned back into the bench as far as possible, wishing I could melt into the wood and disappear.

I couldn't worry about Whitney anymore. She had said the word "we"... we've been there. She had included me and the others. I had to worry about myself now.

"So, you have been there. You and who else?"

Then Whitney surprised me. She stiffened her back and leaned forward. The words proceeded from her mouth with a strength I never imagined she could have.

"It doesn't matter who else was with me because there were never any witches in the cabin. I... we... were only there because certain men in the Community had forced themselves upon us, just as Robbie did that night in the back room of the store. And we ran away, hiding wherever we could!"

The eruptions in the Community Hall were so loud that the cries echoed in my ears. Standing was no longer enough to silence the people. Hayden McVeigh had to raise his hands and actually cry out over the crowd to get them settled from the frenzy they'd riled themselves into.

Once they were again settled and quiet, no one said a word. Each waited with anticipation as Jonathan Alden ripped into the testimony of Whitney Crouse, tearing to shreds every last word concerning Robbie and witches and why she... we... had really gone to the cabins.

He talked about the certainty of witches living in the cabins, although no one had ever actually seen them. He insisted that every girl who had been disobedient enough to venture into the cabins had either directly come into contact with the witches or were at least subconsciously under their evil spell.

Finally, when Whitney could no longer take it, she began to break down. Her face turned a deep shade of red. She began sobbing into cupped hands while vehemently shaking her head back and forth. "Why is this happening... why is this happening?" She said the words over and over again.

"All this is happening because you're a witch!" Jonathon Alden's voice bounced off the walls and filled the heads of those Community members who wanted to believe the accusations as much as he did.

"I love God. I'm not a witch," she insisted. Whitney's voice was so small and soft that I doubt it even reached the ends of the Community Hall. I could barely hear her words from where I sat in the fifth row.

Jonathon looked at Timothy Lane and then back to where Hayden McVeigh was standing. After making eye contact and receiving a slight nod from each of them, Jonathon excused Whitney from the witness stand.

## The Testimony of Alison Flowers

Compared to the intense testimony that Ruth Anne and Whitney had given, Alison's words were surprisingly calm in comparison. This surprised me, considering Alison's outspoken personality.

"What did you see in the back room?" Jonathon asked.

"I walked in on Robbie and Whitney fighting."

"What did you do?" Jonathon asked.

"I tried to stop it."

The rest of her testimony was short and uneventful, and made me wonder if things were going on I knew nothing about. My mind again wandered to the day I'd seen Alison kissing Patrick, and now a thousand different scenarios of what exactly was going on with them filled my imagination. Before I could spend any more time dwelling on the infinite possibilities, Jonathon Alden called Robbie McVeigh to the witness stand.

## The Testimony of Robbie McVeigh

The bandages that had been covering his cuts and bruises were removed, and the wounds were put on display for the entire Community to see.

"What happened to you?" Jonathon asked. "Looks like you've been attacked by a wild animal."

"Could say that," Robbie muttered.

"Tell us why you were in the back room of the Community store."

"I'd spent the last four hours hunting and was hungry. I could smell the venison cooking and went into the store to see if they could spare a bowl."

The rest of what he said soon became nothing but a blur, but I remember this: he was a master showman. From his long, sad face to the trembling of his hands, he described the terror he went through as two young girls, obviously vexed by witches, overwhelmed him and nearly killed him with a knife.

Whitney had been the one who had used the knife. Alison had used her bare hands. And that was why, as we would be told later by the elders, Whitney would receive harsher punishment while Alison would be given a lighter sentence.

"Did I grab hold of them? Yes. I was trying to talk some sense into them. I was trying to save them from their poor choices and bring them back into the fold of God."

Deep sighs of pity for such wayward girls filled the crowded Hall. Above all the commotion, Whitney suddenly stood up and cried out. "It's not true! He's lying!"

Elizabeth McVeigh reached out with large, trembling hands and attempted to grab Whitney and bring her back down to the bench. But Whitney broke free of her grasp and ran to the center of the room.

She pointed a finger at Robbie's face. "You're lying! You tried to rape me! You tried to rape the others as well!"

"You tried to cut off my penis!" he stammered.

"I didn't, but I should have! If you ever come near me again, I will!"

The room erupted. This time with more than mere noise. The unwanted touching and the overwhelming fear that so many of us had kept locked up in our heads for months burst forth from Whitney. Jonathon Alden was the first to grab Whitney and drag her back to the bench.

Robbie closed his eyes and dropped his head. I'd never seen an expression quite like that on his face before. For a moment, I thought he might confess. Then it would all be over. The girls would go home, eventually be married, have families, and forget any of this ever happened. Robbie would get some kind of ridiculously easy punishment like hoeing one of the gardens all by himself. Everyone would talk about how difficult the punishment was and how much he had suffered. I had almost made myself believe it was going to happen. But then he lifted his head and opened his mouth.

"Whitney attacked me like a vicious animal because I told her that she had to go home and not back to the witches."

Again, Community members cried out. But this time, there was anger in their voices. There was pointing of fingers and brutal glares in the direction of Whitney. But Whitney didn't try to defend herself anymore. She must have known it was useless.

# Chapter Ten

We were all sent home under a stark gray sky, so full of fear and strange-shaped clouds that they seemed to be making ugly faces each time I looked up. I was certain the clouds were trying to separate me from God. In their attempt to keep us apart, I feared they would drop hail, snow, and sleet on us before we reached our front door. But the weather held off until after we had eaten dinner.

We had been forbidden to do our chores until after the verdicts were rendered. Duties surrounding the Preparation were temporarily postponed as well. I was left with nothing to do but sit wrapped in a thick blanket as I stared out the front window, mesmerized by the sleet that beat along the panes like tiny shards of glass.

My mother came into the living room carrying a paisley cloth bag stuffed full of yarn and several pairs of different-sized knitting needles. "I've wanted to make an afghan for ages, but never seem to have enough time," she said.

The words were jittery and nervous as they tumbled out of her mouth and landed in the empty spaces in our living room.

She slowly pulled several needles out of the bag. My mother was a good cook but had not excelled at sewing and knitting.

Abigail, however, was a gifted seamstress. Her tiny fingers were nimble and quick, and she had an innate flair for selecting patterns and colors. It quickly became apparent that my mother intended for Abigail and me to knit and that she would simply unroll the yarn.

"Abigail!" she yelled while unloading the bag on the sofa. "Come out and knit with your sister."

She didn't have to tell Abigail twice. Once we started and my hands settled into an easy routine, I was thankful my mother had instructed us to work together. The only activity I enjoyed more would have been working in the greenhouse. But sitting here with Abigail, knitting a blanket that would take the two of us only a few days to complete, was enough to take my mind off what was happening beyond the front door of our tiny house.

That evening, Jada Brewer trudged through several inches of newly fallen snow to deliver the news. It was amazing how quickly she recovered after learning she wouldn't have to testify at the trial.

She stood on our small front porch and knocked. I immediately knew it was her, as I had come to recognize the way several members of the Community knocked. Elizabeth McVeigh pounded on the door as if she were trying to break it down with her clenched fist. Kathleen Alden had a soft, dainty knock that could barely be heard. Jada's knock was a light *tap, tap, tap*, in a perfect rhythmic pattern.

I answered without waiting for my mother. I opened the door to find Jada frowning and shivering on our front steps. She instantly pasted on a smile, but the shivering she couldn't control.

"Come in," I said quickly.

I knew she was bringing us news concerning Whitney and Alison, but I desperately wished she had sent Lynette. I already missed the companionship of my friends.

Jada said hello, then made a beeline to Abigail and the beautiful knitted blanket we had both been working on. Without my mother in the room, she could postpone what would almost certainly be bad news and focus on a pretty little girl with an extraordinary talent for creating gorgeous needlework.

"Your cable work is just exquisite," Jada said. Her stiff, wrinkled fingers gently scanned the thick, cabled stitching. "And the colors are very nice."

"I chose baby blue and cream because it reminds me of the tops of the mountains when they touch the sky."

"Abigail, put the knitting away for today and start your schoolwork," my mother said as soon as she walked into the living room.

I was thankful she had not ordered me to leave as well.

"I have news," Jada said as soon as Abigail had shut our bedroom door.

She quickly explained that a verdict and punishment had been decided for Alison, but they had not yet decided regarding Whitney.

"What's going to happen to Alison?" I blurted out before she had even finished speaking.

"The elders decided that an earth cleansing, mid-level, is appropriate. It will be carried out first thing tomorrow morning and last 24 hours."

My mother gasped, but I didn't make a sound. It wasn't the worst thing that could have happened to Alison.

"I should be going," Jada said. "I have others to inform."

As an elder lady in the Community, she had been given special responsibilities. One of the most important was to deliver messages from house to house that had not been given over the pulpit.

My mother retreated to the kitchen as soon as Jada was gone. I knew she didn't like Alison and wanted desperately to tell me what a bad influence she was. But how could she? After all, it wasn't that long ago that I had been sentenced to a cleansing as well.

I was glad I was alone. It gave me time to watch the snow through the front window. It fell like tiny bits of feathers, soft and fat snowflakes drifting innocently to the ground.

At first, I was confused that Alison's punishment had quickly been decided and Whitney's had not. Yes, Whitney was the one who had wielded the knife, but they had basically been accused of the same things. Then I remembered Alison and Patrick between the leather hide and the barn, the kisses, and the way she had wrapped her arms around him.

I closed my eyes, opened them quickly, and then stared into what had become a blinding snow. But I couldn't unsee what they had done.

Of course, he liked her. That's why she had been spared. Patrick was Hayden's younger brother and a junior elder. He surely influenced the punishments that were handed out.

My anger toward Alison and Patrick melted under a sudden terror that overwhelmed me. If an earth cleansing had been a lighter sentence for Alison, what would happen to Whitney?

***

While we were still anticipating the verdict for Whitney, clouds as dark as night rose over the Community in place of the morning sun. Even though it looked like a blizzard would erupt at any moment, we went about the usual business like clockwork. And the usual business was carrying out the punishment the elders had ordered.

The Community members lined up along the main road as if waiting for a Fourth of July parade. Instead of a parade with fire trucks, decorated floats, and pretty balloons, there was only Alison, escorted to the end of the road by one of the elders.

Jonathon Alden and two teenage boys were waiting with shovels when Timothy Lane brought Alison to the designated site. She stood between the elders as the boys pushed their shovels into the frozen ground and began to dig.

We gathered closer to watch as the discipline was about to be carried out. It was not that everyone perversely enjoyed the punishment of others. We knew we were to come in as close as possible.

We were expected to pay close attention to every detail: the freezing wind on our red faces, clumps of dirt as hard as chunks of ice, and a teenage girl dressed only in overalls and an overcoat. It was to serve as a stark warning to anyone else who decided to wander astray.

With temperatures below freezing, the ground was as hard as a brick. I wondered if mud would have been easier to tolerate. Each of the boys dug with horrific force, struggling and sweating profusely in the cold. Jonathon and Timothy were especially forceful, throwing clumps of frozen ground over their shoulders while grunting and heaving.

I suppose this was done in an attempt to intimidate Alison. If it was, it didn't seem to have the desired effect. Whether it was strength or rebellion that sustained Alison, I couldn't know, but she stood firm and tall as if they didn't even exist.

She never said a word while they continued to dig, piling the dirt into a mound behind the growing hole. She didn't flinch when Elders McVeigh and Alden lifted her by the arms and lowered her into the massive hole.

I had never been so enamored by anyone in all my life as I was with Alison at that very moment. I was still so angry with her about Patrick, yet this strength she possessed impressed me. Or was it only pride? I didn't know. Her expressionless face gave no clues.

"Breathe in and exhale slowly," Jonathon Alden instructed as the dirt was shoveled back in around her waist. "Hold the exhale."

It was the only humanity I saw him display that morning. Even in her defiant silence, I knew Alison was following the elder's instructions. If she didn't, there wouldn't be room for her to breathe. She would suffocate and die.

The only person I watched more closely than Alison was Patrick. He stood along the edge of the crowd next to his wife. For several seconds, I couldn't take my eyes off him. She had willingly kissed him. He had gently held onto her as if he actually cared about her.

When the last clod of dirt had been situated and Alison positioned so she could breathe yet have no possibility of escape, Jonathon Alden nodded his head in satisfaction. He turned and said something to Timothy Lane that no one else could hear. They seemed casual and relaxed as they spoke. I thought Jonathon Alden might even break out into a smile, but then stopped himself. I often wondered, long after that event, what they had said to one another.

The elders turned around and walked away. Then the rest of us followed behind, slowly, methodically. I couldn't move for the longest time. I kept looking at Alison, buried in the ground. But she wouldn't look back at me.

"Come on, let's go," my mother said. She grabbed my arm and pulled.

For twenty-four hours, her head, chest, arms, and hands were all that were exposed above the ground. Thankfully, it was February, and most animals were hibernating for the winter. Unfortunately, it was February, and the temperatures, especially at night, were below freezing. All it would take was one ravenous creature to begin gnawing on fingers and facial features to make those twenty-four hours a living hell.

That night, I was extremely restless. The thought of Alison buried in the dark caused me to pace between my bedroom and the living room. I would stop occasionally and glance out the front window, half expecting to see Alison trudging toward the house, dirt still stuck in her hair and on her face and arms.

I could almost see Alison digging herself out and crawling back to the Community covered in mud and dirt and an angry scowl. But every time I looked out the window, all I could see were the scattered trees bending under the wind and bowing to the emptiness of the dusty road.

"Just go to bed. When you wake up, it will all be over," my mother said.

"Even if everything turns out okay with Alison, Whitney's trouble is only beginning."

She didn't answer but continued to help Abigail with her math homework. Since Sarah Crouse had been the teacher for the Community School, the elders had declared a two-week break until everything was settled with Whitney.

Already, there was talk of another woman in the Community taking over. No matter what happened, elders expected lessons to continue at home.

I kept pacing back and forth until my mother gave me a look that said I was interrupting her lesson on long division. I finally took my nervous energy to my bedroom, turning and forcing a smile in Abigail's direction before closing the door.

"I can't find my wire brush," I said, opening the bedroom door a few minutes later.

"It's on my dresser." My mother didn't look up when she spoke.

I walked into her bedroom and quickly found the brush, but took my time leaving my mother's room. The small closet was slightly open, and I could see each article of clothing neat, orderly, and hanging in its proper place. The shoes were on the floor beneath, each pair snugly beside the others, meticulously pointing in the right direction.

Then my eyes wandered to the small bookshelf by the door. I read the titles of the few books she had brought from Denver. And then, for some reason, I thought of the only other book she owned that was not prominently displayed with the others. The Holy Bible.

It was still where I remembered my mother putting it so many years earlier. In the bottom drawer of her dresser, stuffed between an old picture album and an afghan she never used, was a black King James Bible. I carefully pulled it out, gently holding the leather-bound book.

I held the Bible so my mother couldn't see it when I left her bedroom. But she and Abigail were so immersed in the intensity of long division that she didn't even look up when I walked by. I quickly went to my bedroom, closed the door, situated myself on my bed, and eagerly anticipated this forbidden book.

The pages were crisp, and many were stuck together, indicating the book was old but had rarely been opened. I had no idea where to even begin. I simply opened the Bible and landed somewhere in the Old Testament.

"Zeph...a...niah," I said under my breath. How would I ever figure out who God was, lost somewhere in the Old Testament, struggling to read through books with names I couldn't pronounce? But then I started reading, and what I read took my breath away.

*The Lord hath taken away thy judgments,*
*he hath cast out thine enemy:*
*the king of Israel, even the Lord, is in the midst of thee:*
*thou shalt not see evil anymore.*
*In that day it shall be said to Jerusalem, Fear thou not:*
*and to Zion, Let not thine hands be slack.*
*The Lord thy God in the midst of thee is mighty;*
*he will save, he will rejoice over thee with joy;*
*he will rest in his love, he will joy over thee with singing.*
Zephaniah 3:15-17

It was so amazing that I read it again.

*The Lord hath taken away thy judgments,*
He really isn't judging us all the time?

*He hath cast out thine enemy:*
Oh, how I wanted to believe that.

*the king of Israel, even the Lord, is in the midst of thee:*
I ached for him to be near me.

*thou shalt not see evil anymore.*
I longed to see no more evil.

*In that day it shall be said to Jerusalem, Fear thou not:*
I could hardly imagine a life without fear.

*and to Zion, Let not thine hands be slack.*
There was surely no one weaker than myself.

*The Lord thy God in the midst of thee is mighty;*
I'm glad he said this twice, I needed to hear it.

*he will save, he will rejoice over thee with joy;*
Did he care enough to be glad over me?

*he will rest in his love, he will joy over thee with singing.*
God joys over me? He sings? Amazing.

Without warning, my mother pushed open the door and asked what I was doing.

"Abigail is already done with her math work?" I sputtered.

"What are you doing?" she asked again. She seemed to forget that Abigail even existed.

I told her I was reading the Bible as if it were the most natural thing in the world. But the look on her face was one of sheer panic, perhaps even horror, that I would even think to read the Bible without one of the elders or their wives there to carefully interpret the meaning for me.

"You'll be led astray if you read the Bible yourself," she said sternly. She walked over to take the book out of my hands, but I pulled it away before she could grab it. These words were more precious than gold.

"Hannah, you don't know what you're doing."

I looked down at the Bible, still open, the words *God* and *rejoicing* and *singing* jumping off the pages and swirling around in front of me. "I think I'm just finally beginning to know what I am doing."

The look on my mother's face had shifted from mere annoyance to anger and then fear.

"Tell me you'll at least talk to the elders about what you read? Please? And don't tell anyone you're trying to understand the Holy Scriptures without guidance."

That's what it was really about, what anyone else knew, especially the elders, not misunderstanding what God was trying to tell us.

"Sure," I said. I looked down again and started reading another chapter, pretending she wasn't even in the room.

"You need to get bathed and have your clothes ready," my mother said stiffly. "We need to be ready to gather at the Community Hall first thing in the morning, whenever the decision is made regarding Whitney."

I sighed and closed the Bible. I set it on the dresser and got up to prepare for bed. "We wouldn't want the elders to get upset if we weren't ready to jump every time they called," I said sharply.

She grabbed my arm and jerked me so close that I could feel her breath against my face. Up until that moment, I could never remember my mother grabbing me with such intensity.

"I won't tolerate that kind of disrespect." Her eyes were full of darkness, but the sudden burst of anger subsided, and the fear quickly returned. "Haven't you suffered enough?" she said, barely above a whisper.

She dropped my arm, but I didn't move. I was still standing next to her, my toes nearly touching hers. I had to say the words directly to her face; maybe then she would begin to understand.

"I have to find out what's real and who God is. I'm going to suffocate if I don't."

She looked at me like she understood, but only for a moment, and then she turned and left the room. I had connected with her, but she couldn't overcome the fear. As long as I could hold onto those words I'd just read, I believed I could do anything and that possibly, the fear of what our life was in the Community could be overcome.

# Chapter Eleven

The following morning, only minutes after the sun had risen, the elder women were dispersed throughout the Community, knocking on doors and delivering the order to be at the Community Hall by nine.

I had never known my mind to be so entirely blank and devoid of any rational thought. I dressed, helped Abigail with the breakfast dishes, and told my mother it was time to go.

It was always my mother who was so orderly and would tell us when it was time to leave. This particular morning, she nervously puttered around her bedroom, randomly moving from one place to the next and then making excuses for why she wasn't ready.

"We shouldn't be late," I finally said. My voice sounded strange, like one of the old lady's voices as they tapped and called from the other side of the front door. We quickly gathered our coats and made our way down the main road.

As soon as everyone was gathered in the Community Hall, a dead silence engulfed the building. No one said a word.

When they brought Whitney into the hall, I could feel the deep breaths of everyone around me, sucking the oxygen out of the room. It was as if they were all trying desperately not to act shocked, but they were; we all were. She looked terribly thin and pale. Her large eyes, once a pretty blue, were now a cloudy gray.

Whitney was escorted back to the witness stand to hear the verdict. She was made to wait there, on the platform of the Community Hall, showcased in front of everyone.

Before the verdict and punishment for Whitney were announced, Alison had to be dealt with. When Timothy Lane and Robbie McVeigh brought her into the courtroom, only seconds after Whitney had been brought in, loud gasping again filled the hall. Built-up emotion spilled over the pews in the form of nervous chatter. For the first time I could remember, Hayden McVeigh tolerated uncontrolled noise in the Community Hall.

Alison had been brought straight from the hole she had been buried in. She hadn't been given time to shower, change, or even eat and was still in the same mud-stained, urine-soaked clothes. I found out later that the elders had given her a cup of water, but that was all. She would also lose part of her left ear due to frostbite.

Alison was placed in the front row, directly across from where Whitney was sitting. They looked like two disheveled mannequins, positioned exactly as the elders wanted.

Hayden McVeigh stood in front of the pews between Alison and Whitney. "Let us pray," he said solemnly.

Every time we had ever prayed, I'd always kept my eyes shut. That's what my mother, the elders, and the elders' wives had instructed us to do. Today, I opened my eyes and looked directly at Hayden McVeigh. His eyes were tightly shut, and his facial features were as stiff as stone, except for his mouth.

"Almighty and powerful God, we ask you to come to this place! Bring your justice and dispel the great evil that has tried to overtake us. Amen."

Hayden McVeigh slowly pressed the creases out of his ash-gray suit. He looked across the room at all the solemn faces, but he wouldn't look at Whitney Crouse when he declared, "Guilty! We have found you, Whitney Crouse, guilty of rebellion and witchcraft!"

Gasps and cries of unbridled emotion filled the Community Hall. Alison had been found guilty of rebellion but not of witchcraft.

"I'm not a witch! I'm innocent!" Whitney cried above all the others.

Phil and Sarah Crouse rushed to their daughter but were held back by Patrick and Robbie.

"If she confesses in time, she'll save her immortal soul!" Hayden McVeigh shouted.

But hearing that only caused Sarah Crouse to collapse on the spot. The babies cried for their mother as Phil Crouse attempted to comfort the younger children while at the same time reviving his wife. After Ruth Anne Weber was permitted to examine Sarah, she promptly called for several young men to carry her out of the Community Hall.

I was afraid that I, too, would collapse when Hayden and Patrick slipped ropes around Whitney's arms and waist and practically dragged her to the stairs that led to the basement. It took all my strength just to pull oxygen into my body, one strained breath at a time.

"What's going to happen to her?" Abigail asked. "They haven't sentenced her."

I knew there was no need for formal sentencing. Hayden McVeigh had already read the verse loud and clear during his previous sermons. He had already declared what needed to be done if anyone in the Community was found guilty of witch-craft or consorting with witches. No one said a word about what punishment would befall Whiney Crouse; no one had to, except for a little girl who still didn't understand.

"You don't need to worry about it," our mother said. "The elders will take care of it. They'll know what to do."

My mother still believed that Hayden McVeigh and Jonathon Alden were incapable of any wrong, and somehow, all that was happening existed within the realm of what was good and right.

As soon as we were dismissed, I grabbed Abigail's hand and pulled her out of the Community Hall before she had a chance to hear anyone say out loud what was going to happen to Whit-ney. I didn't look behind to see if my mother was following us. The clickety-click of her old shoes assured me that she was following close behind in the corridor of the Community Hall.

An older child, even one going through the Preparation, was not to be in charge of younger children unless explicitly instructed. This rule was to be closely followed even for something as simple as deciding when to leave a formal gathering.

There was such an uproar inside that no one seemed to notice. I continued to pull Abigail through tangles of people, trying to hold her up, until I realized she was pulling me.

"This way, Hannah," her tiny voice cried as my hand almost slipped from hers. "We're almost home."

The main road was filling with people, their whispering words rising above their heads and blocking out the sun. A gush of cold air revived me and gave me the energy to walk briskly again. My head began to spin when an elderly couple nearby said out loud what I hoped Abigail wouldn't hear.

"They're actually going to put that girl to death," the old man said, shaking his head.

"If she's a witch, she must burn," the old woman said sternly.

Abigail looked up at me with horror in her eyes.

"Let's go home," I heard myself say.

***

My mother quickly shut the door, closed the curtains in the front room, and then fell back on the sofa as if we were all finally safe. I sat down next to her, still breathing hard. Abigail stood right in front of us.

"Are they really going to burn Whitney to death?" Abigail whispered.

"Hush." My mother leaned forward and pressed a finger against Abigail's lips. It was unbearable to even hear the words.

"Something will happen to stop it," I said. "They'll declare some other punishment, or they'll discover new evidence. I just know something will happen."

It was the first time I'd lied in a long time. But after seeing the terror on Abigail's face, I felt I had to say it.

Maybe they didn't officially declare the punishment because the children were in the Community Hall, or it could have been that they wanted us to suffer through this ordeal as long as possible. Whatever the reason, the adults and those going through the Preparation were summoned again the next morning to hear Whitney's sentence.

"The Scriptures are clear," Elder McVeigh said. His voice was stiff and unwavering. "Do not suffer a witch to live." The words sounded strange and hollow. They echoed between the walls, hanging over our heads, ready to pronounce judgment on anyone who dared fight back against an elder and his declaration of punishment.

"Within twenty-four hours, the witch will be burned."

It was so quiet in the Community Hall, I was afraid the vacuum of silence would suck us all into eternity. Then a gust of wind picked up outside the window. It was enough to keep us all here on earth, at least for now. Then the whimpering started. It was Mrs. Crouse, the shock melting the silence and emerging as mournful cries, and finally erupting into a full-blown wail that outcried the wind.

"No... No," she said. "It can't be right. She's my little girl!"

Hayden McVeigh refused to make eye contact with anyone in the room, especially Whitney's screaming mother. His gaze stretched beyond the length of the Community Hall. I suppose he thought he could see right into eternity, the eternity Whitney was quickly heading for.

"Take her away," he said in a gentle voice. It was the most frightening thing I think I'd ever heard up to that point in my entire life.

Jonathon Alden took hold of Whitney's left arm, ready to escort her down to the basement where she would again be held until the sentence was carried out. Her legs, looking strange and tangled under her frail body, collapsed under the weight of her sobs. Timothy Lane quickly stepped up and grabbed hold of her right arm.

As soon as Whitney was taken away, everyone began to immediately disperse. I hadn't heard any of the elders dismiss us. Perhaps they hadn't, but once the stampede to leave the Community Hall started, it couldn't be stopped.

My mother began walking faster as we approached our house. I purposely lagged behind. I looked up at the sky, gray and thick as wool, and sent out a prayer. It was the most sincere prayer I had ever prayed in my life. I whispered, "Dear Jesus, God Almighty, if you're really there, if you're listening, send me a sign."

And then I stopped. I was afraid God would be angry that I was so demanding. But the God I was increasingly coming to know in the Bible would want me to cry out to him. I was certain of it. So I became even bolder. "God, if every single thing I've read about you is true, save me from the Community. Make a way for me to leave."

"Hannah, hurry up," my mother yelled from the front doorstep. I began to run. At that moment, I believed that the God I had read about in the Bible was not the same God who was preached about in the Community. And which was the true God would determine how my prayer was answered.

# Chapter Twelve

There was a single chair in the entire greenhouse. It was a basic wooden chair that didn't look the least bit comfortable. Lately, whenever Gretchen was here, she would sit in it and watch me work. Being almost six months pregnant, she was becoming increasingly tired.

I don't think I had ever sat in that chair, even once, until today. And I quickly discovered that I was wrong about the chair. It was comfortable. After nearly an hour of work, it felt soothing to fall back into its simple wooden frame.

I lowered my aching body, feeling the wood against my spine and thinking how comfortable a block of wood actually felt. Instead of standing over the top of most of the plants in the greenhouse, I was now at eye level. I'd never really seen them from this vantage point, and it was amazing how incredibly beautiful they were.

To my left, I saw several rows of lettuce, spinach, and green onions. These vegetables were constant staples in our diet. Basil, dill, thyme, and sage grew in tiny pots lined up in rows along wooden tables. Jada Brewer could make the most delicious recipes with those few simple herbs and a little chicken broth.

Then I looked up at the tomatoes growing from hanging baskets. There were long, thick vines with succulent tomatoes, many already beginning to ripen. That's when I noticed something was wrong.

The last hanging pot in the second row had obviously been tampered with, tampered with in such a way that saying it had been vandalized would not have been too strong a word. Revived with energy, I stood up and walked toward the ravished plant. Before I could get to the hanging tomatoes, I saw the shadow of a man standing behind the table full of green beans.

Confused, I thought maybe someone standing outside the small window was casting shadows on the inside of the greenhouse. Perhaps it was Jonathon or Hayden lurking around outside, spying on me to make sure I was constantly working.

Then I saw his arm move, almost imperceptibly. It was not a mere shadow but flesh. It was the dark flesh of a man who would not have been a member of the Community.

Fear and confusion melded into one unsettling emotion. I screamed and backed away in the same instant, crashing against a table full of lettuce, radishes, and buckets half full of water.

Containers with seedlings and metal buckets containing dirt clanged together in a sloppy, wet mess as I attempted to steady myself. In all that time, this man had neither moved nor made a sound. Maybe he was so frightened that he couldn't move, or maybe the elders were right, and what I saw wasn't even a human being.

Then he leaned forward enough that the light of the kerosene lamp illuminated the left side of his face and body. I was definitely looking at a man. A Black man. I hadn't seen a person of another race for years. Even when we were in Denver, the people who lived in our neighborhood and attended our school district were almost entirely white.

His hair was wild and unruly, and his shirt was ragged and torn. And he was painfully thin. But most frightening of all were his eyes. They were wide and glassy, the only thing about him that seemed to move. His eyes twitched back and forth in rapid, jerky motions.

"Who are you?" I said sharply, thinking how strange my voice sounded.

He didn't say a word. He remained perfectly still behind the green bean plants. There wasn't a door behind him – no way out except through me. Fear had taken over, and I was no longer operating on conscious thought.

"Are you a witch?" I suddenly heard myself say. I said the words loud and strong. I don't know why I said that. It must have been a subconscious thought spilling out.

Then he smiled. It was slight, barely there, and completely unexpected. He acted like he was confused, which was then followed by what I suspected was amusement. "No, I'm not a witch," he answered plainly. "I'm just a man."

His voice was deeper and stronger than I had expected for someone who looked so weak and underfed.

"Who are you? What do you want?"

He stretched his back and relaxed a bit. I could tell he wasn't as frightened of being discovered as he had been a few seconds earlier. And I wasn't as frightened of him for some reason. I suppose if he was going to hurt me, he probably would have done it by now.

"My name is Ross. I just need someplace to stay for a while."

Now, I was the one who was confused. "Are you homeless? Why would you be out here in the middle of nowhere?"

He sighed. He seemed annoyed that I was asking so many questions. "It's a long story, but the short of it is I'm injured. I need a warm place to recuperate and some food while I'm here."

I studied him as quickly and carefully as I could without staring for too long. He was dirty and ragged, but he didn't look hurt. "What's wrong with you? You don't look injured to me."

He carefully stepped out from behind the table. Slowly reaching up toward his chin, he unzipped the long fleece jacket he was wearing that hung nearly down to his knees. A few inches above his left knee was a bloody spot that had seeped through the gray sweatpants he was wearing.

It was obvious he had wrapped several layers of cloth or bandaging underneath. But the wound had already soaked through to the outer layer of his sweatpants.

"What happened to you? Why are you here instead of at a hospital?"

"I've been shot. Like I said, it's a long story. I just need someplace to stay for a few weeks."

"Is the bullet still in your leg?"

"No. It went through the side of my thigh at an angle. I suppose it's what they would call a superficial wound. But it bled a lot, and it's going to take a while to heal. It starts bleeding every so often if I move around too much."

While I was trying to decide whether I should allow him to stay, evaluating the almost endless scenarios and countless complications, Ross offered his own plan.

"I'll make you a deal. I'll take care of everything in here. I'll do all the watering and fertilizing, and I'll do it at night so no one will notice me. I'll sleep during the day."

I started shaking my head before he even finished speaking. "I actually like working here. It's about the only thing about my life I do enjoy." I wasn't sure why I said that. But then the conversation shifted, and he was now asking about me.

"What is this place?" he asked, acting as if he had stumbled upon some nether world that didn't exist in modern society. But, of course, that was exactly what he had done.

"This is our Community."

He finally stepped out from the shadows and narrowed his eyes. "What kind of Community?"

I'd never been asked to describe who we were, and I found it difficult to put into words. Were we religious according to the standards of others? Were we preppers or survivalists?

"We're a group of people trying to follow God while living naturally away from the big city. That's all."

He nodded, though I'm sure he didn't completely understand. "All I'm asking is that you let me sleep here and eat a little food until I figure out what I'm going to do. Just give me a few weeks, time for my leg to heal, and then I'll be on my way."

He didn't seem willing to tell me much about himself, and I certainly didn't want to go into detail about my own life and the world he had stumbled upon. But this man intrigued me – this strange Black man from the outside world I'd been forced to leave behind years earlier.

As long as no one knew he was here, I couldn't see how I was doing anything wrong. How could it be wrong to help a man, to give him food and shelter when he was hurt?

"Okay, I'll let you stay here and help you, for a little while."

He smiled, and his protruding teeth burst forth from under his thick lips.

"But don't do all the work. You can do the weeding, but save the watering for me. It's my favorite part. And you can't let anyone else know you're here. They wouldn't let you stay."

He quickly nodded, still smiling. "Sure," he said.

"Don't eat more than a few vegetables. I'll bring you something else to eat every day."

He again agreed. "I do need just one more thing," he said softly. It was obvious he was afraid to ask.

"What?" I instantly thought he would want access to some kind of technology, such as a phone, a computer, or maybe even the chance to watch television. Any of that was out of the question in the Community.

"Do you have any antibiotics? Maybe some first aid cream or some fresh bandages?"

I suddenly felt guilty for not thinking to offer him those things on my own. "We have natural remedies and herbs we use for wounds. I can bring you some things either later tonight or tomorrow morning."

He looked relieved. "Thanks. I really appreciate it."

"You can sleep in the utility closet. It's as large as an average bathroom. There are blankets on the shelf, and it stays pretty warm in there. And no one hardly ever goes in there but me."

As I led him back to the closet, I felt an unusual sense of excitement. There was someone here from the real world, some-one who was all mine to talk to and spend time with.

But the anticipation of something exciting and different in my life vanished at the thought of the Community and the elders, and what would happen if anyone else found out this man was hiding in the greenhouse.

While he was situating himself in the utility closet, I attempt-ed to go about my work. But after finding a stranger hiding behind the green bean plants, it was nearly impossible to con-centrate.

I was certain I poured more than twice the amount of water needed on the cauliflower. I think I might have even forgotten to water the lettuce altogether. My usual ability to mix and mea-sure manure and compost into fertilizer like a trained chemist disappeared as I randomly tossed clumps of dead leaves around the herbs.

I was almost finished with my haphazard care of the plants when Ross emerged from the utility room. "Thank you so much for allowing me to stay here. It's even warmer in the closet than those cabins I was staying in."

I instantly forgot about finishing my work. "You were staying in the cabins? The cabins that are about a quarter mile past the meadow?"

"Yes, those cabins. Do the people who live here own them?"

"No. We own the land up to the edge of where the cabins were built. I think the county owns the land they're on now."

I was going to ask if he'd started the fire, but before I had the chance, he started talking again. "I'm sorry, I don't think you told me your name."

"My name is Hannah."

"Thank you, Hannah." He smiled again and then returned to the utility closet.

When I finally left the greenhouse, a light, freezing rain was falling over the Community. The freezing rain against my face slapped me back into reality and reminded me of what I'd completely forgotten about during the last hour – Whitney. As much as I cared about what happened to Whitney and as guilty as I felt for being able to briefly forget about her, I relished the temporary solace that had managed to find me.

I looked up into the gray, icy sky and whispered. "I don't know what this is all about, but thank you."

STAZ

# Chapter Thirteen

We had been instructed to do our work as if everything were normal. Pushing wheelbarrows while properly bundled in gloves, scarves, and coats, we gathered the daily ration of wood. I purposely lagged behind for quite some time before finally telling Alison to slow down.

When Lynette and Katie had wandered into a wooded area, Alison and I were left alone in the clearing. She was still walking but had not yet reached the edge of the woods. Before she was hidden behind a thorny patch of bushes, the words found a way to crawl past my fear.

"About a week ago, I saw you by the barn... with Patrick."

Alison slowed down again but didn't completely stop. "You saw me what?" she said without looking back. She had to know what I meant, but she would make me say it anyway.

I came right behind her and then stopped. "I saw you kissing Patrick, that's what."

She spun around to face me. There wasn't surprise on her face, only anger. "I was kissing him. But it's not what you're thinking."

"I didn't even say what I was thinking."

She looked toward the woods to see if Lynette or Katie had heard what we were saying. They certainly would have come back out if they had. "I was having trouble with the leather piece I was working on. I thought it was ruined, and he helped me fix it. You know the trouble we can get into if our Preparation training doesn't go as planned."

I understood, but she still hadn't explained why she kissed Patrick.

"He saved me from getting a minor punishment. I was so grateful that I kissed him. Of course, he hung on longer than he should have. That wasn't my fault. It was something that just got out of hand."

She turned around and started walking toward the woods again as if everything was completely settled. I wasn't sure if what she'd told me was the truth or not, but I knew I wasn't going to get anything else out of her. Then I suddenly felt guilty. Considering what was about to happen in the Community, something as insignificant as a kiss meant nothing.

***

The next morning, I woke early, before my mother or sister. I went through my morning routine of washing and dressing and then came out to the kitchen to make breakfast. I was constantly watching the clock, feeling an abnormal need to know the time.

The truth was, I wanted the morning to last forever. I hoped that somehow time would stop and we'd forever be trapped in our usual morning routine. The unknown terror about to unfold was so frightening that I couldn't bear the thought of time moving forward.

During the next hour, I worked in the greenhouse. Ross had recently eaten and was sleeping. While becoming so immersed in pruning, weeding, and watering, I managed to keep my mind devoid of any thoughts regarding Whitney.

I knew very little about who God was, but I sensed He was here, and I believed He was happy that I was taking care of His creation. I had actually experienced several minutes of calm and contentment before my mother came into the greenhouse, calling my name.

She knew she was to knock, but she didn't. The trembling in her voice caused me to forget that I was angry at her for not doing so. But then, I suddenly remembered why she was here and what it was time for. I tried desperately not to listen to her.

"Hannah, it's time to leave," she said stiffly.

The beets are absolutely beautiful. They were resilient plants that were easy to grow, easy to harvest, and good to eat. Just add a little salt, pepper, and butter, and they are delicious.

"Hannah, please don't make us late!"

I loved melons and sweet corn, but these didn't do well in the short growing season, and so they were never planted. The easiest were radishes and onions. I was certain those vegetables could grow almost anywhere.

"Hannah! You have to come, or the elders will come for you!"

I took a long, deep breath. I could not allow myself to cry. So I focused on each moment in itself... the slamming of the greenhouse door... my mother taking hold of my hand as if I were a small child again.

Once we were out on the main road, the tranquility of the greenhouse was sucked into the maddening silence of the empty road. The only sound was the shuffling of shoes across the frozen dirt. Even the wind was quiet. The clouds in the sky were stiff and unwavering. They hung like dreary gray blankets, too heavy to move. The sun disappeared into the depths of an endless universe, unwilling to look down and watch what was about to happen. Even the birds refused to sing. Nature was trembling, waiting to see what mankind would do next.

Everyone was coming out of their homes and places of work at the same time. Their heads were lowered. There were no faces. Everywhere, there were shuffling feet, people moving without looking, without talking. I wanted to scream. I wanted to demand that everyone open their mouths and talk, but I was also unable to speak.

My mother stopped at the front of our house, called for Abigail, and then waited for her to join us. The sight of Abigail putting on her hat and gloves as if we were getting ready to take a leisurely stroll to the general store gave me the strength to open my mouth. The words fell out like pebbles splashing into an icy stream.

"Tell her to go back inside. She doesn't need to come to this."

My mother looked at me as if I'd said something obscene. "The elders have ordered that every person in the Community is to witness what is about to take place."

I must have been dragging my feet, not moving fast enough. My mother was practically pulling me along while Abigail walked briskly beside us.

I was praying inside my head and wondering if God could hear me and if it even counted as a prayer. People screamed in their heads all the time. If God were listening, He must have known that I couldn't possibly scream any louder or my head would explode.

It's less than half a mile to the north meadow, and we're all walking at such a brisk pace that we'll be there within minutes. When the tree comes into my line of vision, I'm certain the sight of it will blind me with all its massive glory.

The branches are bent and rugged, like a man with a dozen arms, holding each one in a bodybuilder pose with clenched fists. I look to the left, and then to the right, at all the mindless people walking silently toward the tree.

Men, women, children, and babies, we're trudging out into the burnt, barren field where a lone tree stands, waiting for us all. Beautiful, proud, and stoic, it stands in the midst of a bitter Wyoming winter.

Whitney was brought alongside the procession in the Community van, her ashen face peering through the back window. I can still remember that face, though I can't even begin to describe her expression. The only thing I can compare it to is the way a baby animal would look locked in a cage after its mother had been taken away. Those eyes, so deep and empty, are beyond what I can even bear to remember now.

The driver, Robbie McVeigh, drove so slowly that the van barely passed the people on the road as they continued to walk. It gave everyone time to look into the back of the van and stare into the face of Whitney Crouse.

I never found out for sure, but I assumed that she was tied to the back window. She must have been held there by ropes, chains, or whatever had been placed in the back of the van. I couldn't imagine she would stay there, looking out at everyone in the Community, unless she had been forced.

The moment the van doors opened and Whitney saw the tree and the kindling and the straw stacked around the trunk, she began to scream. Hayden McVeigh covered her mouth with his large, fleshy hand. She must have bitten his hand because he instantly pulled it away.

"No! Noooooo!" she cried.

They were long, hideous screams. Her voice sounded as if she were already on fire. It was only a matter of seconds before the crowd joined in and formed a chorus of unbearable sounds. Gasping and crying, it all came forth at once as the crowd erupted into a frenzy.

"I'm not a witch! I swear it!" she cried as they dragged her kicking and screaming to the tree.

It took four men to tie her to the tree. Her arms, legs, and waist were so secure she couldn't move anything below her neck. Her head twisted and turned around like a toy bobblehead.

The elders didn't even attempt to control the screaming crowd. Other than keeping everyone a safe distance from the tree, they seemed content to let chaos unfold. Without looking at me, Katie grabbed hold of my hand and squeezed. I hadn't realized she had even been standing next to me.

"Hold me up," she whispered.

While I held Katie, I held onto my mother's coat with my other hand.

Hayden McVeigh, Jonathon Alden, Timothy Lane, and Patrick McVeigh stood somberly around the tree. Whitney, so small compared to these large, overbearing men, had become strangely silent.

I tried to imagine the thoughts going through Whitney's head, but my mind went blank and a wave of vast emptiness surrounded me. Perhaps there was nothing left but emptiness inside Whitney as well. Her eyes were as blank as the sky until each of the men stepped forward and held up a match.

All four of them lit the match and buried it in the straw at the same time. Accountability had to be dispersed. They were sharpshooters at a firing range. Each had to be able to soothe their conscience with the belief that someone else's flame had killed her.

But no, it really wasn't that way. It only had to appear that way. Each one of them believed he was doing God's work. Each one would have gladly lit the match without any help from the others.

Once the fire started, Whitney stared intently at the flames coming toward her. The hypnotizing dance of orange and yellow flickers of light was a mercy. The flames moved slowly at first, but something must have ignited it about halfway toward the tree. An extra dry branch, a low gust of wind, whatever it was, the fire erupted into an inferno less than a yard from her feet.

"God Almighty," a man said behind me.

"Lord have mercy," a woman cried.

I looked at my mother and then down at the ground. "I can't watch."

She pulled my head around by the hair.

"If you don't watch, God only knows what they'll do to you," she said in a low, frightening voice.

I lifted my head but tilted my eyes slightly downward so I could no longer see Whitney. I could only see the branches, the smoke, and the flames rising around her legs. And I believed that as long as I didn't actually see her burning, I'd be okay, that somehow I'd survive this.

When the fire finally reached her, she let forth the most horrific, unbearable wail I'd ever heard in my life. But nothing on this earth could compare to the smell of burning flesh. The detestable odor crawled up my nose one breath at a time.

My mind must have blocked out all conscious thought after that because I don't remember seeing or hearing anything of significance, only the hellish smell. It was then that I knew beyond a doubt that hell really did exist. Evil had clawed its way up from the depths of the earth and settled among the thorns and the branches and the withering grass.

The last thought I had was wondering if Whitney would go to heaven or hell. Then my mother finally pulled my arm, and time started again.

"It's over. We have to go now."

That's when I looked up and saw the charred remains of Whitney Crouse.

## Counselor

I'm in the chair, hunched over, my head between my knees.

"Just breathe in," the counselor says softly. "Now exhale."

We did that for several minutes until I was able to lift my head again.

I had not consciously remembered what Whitney had looked like at the time of her death until that moment.

"If I hadn't known what it was, it probably wouldn't have looked that bad. I would have seen a black chunk, something looking almost like an empty, burned-out log," I say. "But I did know what it was."

With a finger to her lips, the counselor tells me to hush and only to keep breathing. What a dead body looks like after being burned is too much for words, at least for now.

"Just look at her and then walk away," the counselor says.

I'm to face my memory of her dead, burnt body, look at it, remember it, *and then just walk away?* But now that I've remembered, I'm afraid I'll never forget. The image, like the scent of death itself, is seared into the innermost crevices of my brain forever.

Then, the counselor asks me to describe what my mother wore that day.

"What?"

"What was your mother wearing? Tell me what color her shirt was and how her hair was done."

This is all so strange. I have to concentrate, really think about it, to remember such insignificant details. "Umm, blue, a sky-blue blouse," I say. "That was my mother's favorite color. And her hair was back in a loose ponytail that swept over her shoulders when she walked. She almost always wore her hair that way."

Then I stop and look at the counselor, and I almost cry. For a few sweet seconds, I had forgotten. The image of Whitney's burned body had left my conscious thought. Of course, that had been her exact plan. By asking seemingly unimportant, mundane questions, she had relieved me of the pain, if only temporarily.

"It will get better with time," she says evenly. "It will take a lot of time, and it won't be easy. But it will happen."

We are both quiet for what seems like a long time. I can hear the assistant in the waiting room meticulously typing into her computer. The muted drone of her fingers clicking against the keyboard is soothing. It's a relief to have something so mundane and meaningless occupying space in my head.

"What are you thinking?" the counselor says.

"I know that there truly is evil in the world."

She sighs. It sounds deep and mournful. Then she says, "But greater is He that is in you than he that is in the world."

# Chapter Fourteen

The cottonwood tree, in all its magnificent glory, still didn't burn. I wanted to see it and stand next to it, but I wasn't sure if I would be comforted in the presence of the tree or terribly frightened. I didn't have a choice, at least for the time being.

The elders had announced that we weren't allowed to leave our homes for twenty-four hours. We were to think and meditate on what had happened at the Burning Tree, why it had to happen, and to make sure we didn't make the same mistakes and fall into the same terrible sins that had destroyed Whitney.

"Eat your cereal," my mother said. "You hardly ate any dinner."

Abigail picked up her bowl of cereal and sat down next to me at the table. She sat so close to me that the rough edges of her overalls scraped against my arm when she leaned to take a bite.

She couldn't stand to be by herself now. When we slept, she couldn't stay on her side of the bed but was constantly touching me, either an arm or a leg, or the side of her face was resting somewhere on me. Even when she went to the bathroom, she kept the door slightly open so she could see or at least hear us in the house.

We could both see through the front window from where we were sitting. I took one bite of the cereal drenched in milk and then put my spoon down. Suddenly, I realized I didn't want to eat another bite. My stomach twisted into knots, and I knew breakfast would end up as useless as dinner.

I closed my eyes, relishing the empty darkness in my head. When I opened them again, I could see Phil and Toby Crouse trudging along the dirt road in front of our house.

Less than twenty-four hours after the burning of Whitney Crouse, the elders gave the family permission to retrieve the remains. A light mist had permeated the north meadow since sunrise this morning, and by the time Phil Crouse and his eldest son made the journey to the meadow, a freezing rain had started that would continue sporadically for the remainder of the day.

I diverted my eyes without moving an inch. I didn't want Abigail to look out the front window. The moment they were gone from view, I excused myself from the table and went back to my bedroom.

I took out my mother's Bible, the one I had permanently taken from her bedroom and kept hidden in my bottom dresser drawer under layers of heavy nightwear and thermal underwear. I suspected she would never miss it since she didn't read it. So far, I was right.

I grabbed one of my old school books and sat on my bed with the quilt partially covering my legs. I held the Bible in such a way that I could easily push it under the blankets and pretend I was reading the school book if my mother should come in unexpectedly.

I opened the Bible, looked down, and began reading what I saw.

*For I am persuaded, that neither death, nor life, nor angels, nor principalities, nor powers, nor things present, nor things to come, Nor height, nor depth, nor any other creature, shall be able to separate us from the love of God, which is in Christ Jesus our Lord.*

Romans 8:38-39

I kept reading through Romans 9, finally stopping after I read the first few verses of chapter 10. The words, which told about the Israelites being zealous for God, but their zeal was not based on knowledge, struck a deep nerve. Reading on, I discovered how they had tried to be saved by the law, by being good, instead of by faith in Christ.

Of course, we should try to be good. I knew somehow that was still true. But I also knew that endless rules and traditions, and trying to do good on our own, would never be enough.

I closed the Bible and quickly returned it to my bottom drawer. I rarely read more than one chapter at a time, sometimes only a few verses at one time. There was so much to think about in even a few verses that reading much more was overwhelming. I had to take it in one word, one thought at a time, meditating on the words that this book had told me came from the heart of God, delivered through the hands of men.

If I hadn't been looking out the back window at that particular moment, I might have missed it. But when my eye caught the movement of something yellow, I walked closer to the bedroom window. I pulled the curtain open far enough to see what was unfolding in the backyard a few houses away from ours.

Phil Crouse, in a yellow shirt and old denim overalls, stood in his backyard with a shovel in his hand. His son, Toby, stood next to him and watched as he dug into the solid earth. Somewhere between the time I had seen Phil and Toby walking past our front window and the moment I looked and saw them standing in their backyard, Sarah had joined them.

Sarah and Toby stood like statues, unwavering, even as a brisk wind wound its way between the houses and through the backyards. Phil, however, was working quickly and intently. With even, methodical motions, he removed one shovelful of dirt at a time. I felt a chill when I saw the cloth bag lying on the ground next to Sarah Crouse. I knew instinctively it was Whitney's remains.

I watched as Phil Crouse settled into his rhythmic routine. The shovel went down into the earth, then up and out, the thick clods of dirt tossed into a heap a few feet away. In and out, the same rhythm, my heart beating faster as the hole grew deeper. As the minutes passed, I could see Phil Crouse leaning further into the ground, the shovel digging farther and farther into the earth.

Without thinking, my hand reached for the handle on the window. I slowly cranked the window open just a few inches, but enough to hear the shovel ripping into the ground. Other than a few groans when he lifted a particularly large chunk of soil, Phil didn't make a sound. Sarah and Toby were not only silent, but each was motionless.

Phil's arms were like machinery on an assembly line. The same parts moved over and over again in the same way, while other parts didn't move at all. When he reached what appeared to be somewhere between two and three feet, he laid the shovel on the ground beside him. When he lifted the cloth sack, I thought my racing heart would suddenly stop beating.

I tried to imagine Whitney inside that bag. Her beautiful face and long, silky hair completely turned to ash.

Of course, the elders weren't there. There would be no official funeral service, no grand speeches of entering the pearly gates into realms of eternal bliss. The elders believed that Whitney would burn forever in eternity and thus would have no part in her burial.

I could barely watch as he dropped the bag into the earth and then crumbled over the top of it. As he began to wail for his baby girl, looking as if he were ready to crawl into the grave and cover himself alongside her, Sarah remained silent. She was an empty shell, frozen in place as he cried uncontrollably.

From where I was standing, I could see Toby gently holding his mother's hand. While she let him grab hold of her, she didn't respond. His eyes started blinking in rapid succession until they closed for good.

I was so mesmerized by the intensity of what was happening only yards outside of my bedroom window that I jumped when my mother placed her hand on my shoulder.

"What are you doing?" She looked over my shoulder and then quickly backed away. "Close that window and draw the curtains," she demanded.

I did as I was instructed, but was immediately angry. "What's wrong with watching? The elders didn't say we couldn't."

"You're not watching; you're spying."

I ran past her and began putting on my coat and gloves.

"Where are you going?"

"To the greenhouse. I have work to do."

"You're not allowed to go to the greenhouse." My mother's voice was filled with more concern than indignation.

Again, I did as I was instructed. I wanted to be rebellious and defy every rule and order I'd ever been given. But I didn't have the strength.

"Take off your coat and sit down. I want you and Abigail to finish the knitting."

I had completely forgotten about the blanket. The thought of working on something so warm and beautiful with Abigail by my side gave me the motivation to pull off my coat and sit down in the front room.

My mother arranged everything. She called Abigail, pulled out the partially finished blanket with the needles still in place, and began unwinding yarn as I maneuvered the needles one stitch at a time.

***

The following morning, all restrictions were lifted, the Preparation had resumed, and we were all to go about our lives as if nothing had happened. I pasted on my plastic face before I left the house and ventured out into the Community.

The only thing that kept me sane was knowing that I would work in the greenhouse, and most likely I would be alone. Gretchen had told me several days earlier that she had an appointment with Ruth Anne and would not be in to see me.

I headed to the back, past the vegetables that took up most of my time, beyond the tiny clay pots full of herbs, and straight to the last few rows of tables full of blooming flowers. The flowers were not necessities, so I was only allowed a little time each week to care for them. Despite my neglect, they were beautiful. The lavender flowers had already sprung up several inches, with hints of color coming into bloom.

The wild strawberries, with their soft white petals and tufts of yellow center, would produce fruit after they were transplanted in a few months. It was then that I realized someone else had been taking care of the flowers and the containers of early fruit. Obviously, Ross was watering, weeding, and caring for them in my absence.

Then I wondered if he was even still here. I quickly walked to the utility room, thinking how much had transpired in only a few short days. I gently tapped on the door, but there was no answer.

For a second, I thought he was gone. Perhaps he had healed faster than we both had anticipated. Maybe he knew what had happened and decided that staying anywhere but here was better. I tapped one more time.

"Ross?"

It felt strange to say his name out loud. Then I heard someone moving around inside and realized he'd been sleeping. It surprised me how relieved I was that he was still here.

I backed away as he stepped out of the utility closet, his clothes wrinkled and his eyes full of sleep. He tilted his head and looked at me like he didn't recognize me. "It's good to see you," he said.

I was drawn to Ross like a magnet, drawn to another human being who was not from the Community I could bear my troubled soul to. I opened my mouth and the words began to spill out, sloppy and jagged. "It's good to see you, too."

When I finally reached him, he grabbed hold of my arms.

"What happened to that girl?" he said. His leg was bleeding again, but he didn't seem to notice. "I saw a girl, a pretty girl with long brown hair, screaming. I looked out the window. I know I shouldn't have, but the screaming was awful."

He stopped for a moment and looked at me. I'll never know what he saw on my face. I imagine pure terror because it took him a moment to catch his breath and speak again.

"I saw them load her in the back of a van. And the people followed it out of town."

He looked out the window again as if the howling wind were conjuring up memories of what he saw. "What happened to her?" he said in a whisper.

"They punished her," I said.

"How?" he said, moving back toward me.

I already knew that he knew how and that he was only waiting for me to confirm it. But the words were stuck in my throat, thicker than the smoke that had risen from the Burning Tree.

The analytical portion of my brain seemed to function independently from the rest of my mind. While my emotions ran wild, my mouth sputtered out something that actually sounded halfway logical. "She was given the punishment that the elders said the Bible prescribed."

I had been so afraid for so long that I didn't realize until attempting to explain it to an outsider just how ludicrous it all was.

"Punished how? Exactly how was she punished?"

I quickly tried to calculate in my head how far the greenhouse was from the north meadow and the Burning Tree. It was at least a quarter mile away. If he was inside the greenhouse when she was put to death, would he have heard anything? Could he have smelled anything?

I opened my mouth, but I couldn't bring myself to say out loud what had happened. "I... I probably shouldn't talk about it. I don't think you would understand anyway."

"Hannah." It was the first time he had said my name. "I know it's not your fault what's happening here, so I'm not blaming you. You've got to tell me what happened to that girl."

"There's no fault and no one to blame. It's just that..." I was breathing hard, fighting back tears, but it was useless. He had stopped walking toward me, but his hands were reaching out.

His long, thin hands engulfed mine, and I suddenly felt safe enough to cry.

"They burned her to death," I cried. "They burned her..."

I could feel the hairs on his arms stand up, but he didn't let go of me.

"You mean the elders in the Community, they did it?"

I nodded my head, my hands still cradled in his arms. "They ordered it, and they did it."

"But why?"

"They said she was a witch and that they had to save the rest of us. They had to purge the sin from the Community. If you're not a person of faith, you wouldn't understand."

Suddenly, he pulled back and let out a long sigh. "I am a person of faith, even though I haven't lived like it for a long time."

Despite the horrible thing that had happened to Whitney, we had suddenly shifted course and were talking about him and the things that had happened in his life.

"What do you mean?" It was my turn to pry him open one painful question at a time.

He sat down on a crate and stared down at his tattered shoes. "You know, everyone does bad things, even when they believe in God."

I sat next to him without saying a word, hoping he'd keep talking.

"I've always believed in God, accepted Christ, and attended church with my grandmother when I was younger. I even thought about going into the ministry while I was in high school."

"What happened?" I asked.

"My dad died, and my whole life went crazy. I hung out with a bad crowd, stopped going to church, and started doing drugs. It's amazing how quickly things can slip out of control, and you don't even realize how bad it's getting when you're caught up in it all."

I wasn't sure if he was still talking about himself or trying to tell me what had gone wrong in my life. Maybe both.

"I kept telling myself I was going to get out next week, next month, but it never happened. Several years went by, and it still never happened."

He stopped talking. It was as hard for him to talk about what happened in his life as it was for me to talk about what was happening here.

"You have to leave this place," he said, barely above a whisper.

I was thinking of a way to tell him, yes, I know. I desperately want to, but it's impossible. Then I heard footsteps coming around the east side of the greenhouse. I could see the blurry figure of Gretchen Lane through the thick plastic window covering.

"Hurry! You've got to get back in the utility room."

He walked as quickly as possible, but with an injured leg, the best he could do was limp briskly. He was inside the closet, covering himself with blankets before she had stepped through the door, but I had to make sure any trace that he was here was completely gone. I quickly scanned the area he'd been standing in for anything that was out of place; even a drop of blood from his wound would have been suspicious.

When I turned around, Gretchen was already heading past the rows of cauliflower and broccoli. Once she made it to the tables with green beans, where she could clearly see the flowers, she stopped and smiled. She rarely smiled, and I was amazed by how pretty she actually was.

"Everything looks good," she said. She slowly nodded and looked around in every direction. "You're getting a lot accomplished in the few hours you're here each day."

I smiled in appreciation. "I thought you had an appointment with Ruth Anne," I said.

"She was up half the night tending to a sick baby. I'll be seeing her tomorrow."

"We've got to make a new batch of fertilizer today, right?" I said quickly.

"Yes," she said. "Let's get to work."

# Chapter Fifteen

I woke the next morning to a crystalline sky, as clear and pure as any I could remember since living in Wyoming. Standing at the window, still in my nightgown, I realized how incredibly hungry I was. I had eaten very little during the last several days, and I could feel my ribs protruding through the cotton nightdress I was wearing. My physical needs had finally overtaken my emotional state, and I hurried to the kitchen.

I fried three eggs, smothered them in onions, and stuffed them all between two thick slices of bread. I devoured the massive sandwich in less than five minutes.

When my stomach was full, I finally thought of Ross. I hadn't taken him anything for a few days and could only imagine how hungry he was.

I scoured the cabinets and the small ice box on the back porch for anything edible that wouldn't be missed. I found two small potatoes and a package of frozen green beans partially hidden under a layer of ice in the box.

Then I cut two thin slices of beef from the large roast my mother had prepared for the week. None of it would be missed, and together, it would make a good meal for Ross.

My mother was at the Community Center teaching several girls in the Preparation how to improve their cooking skills. As her daughter, I was not allowed in her group, but it was just as well. Everything about cooking and baking my mother knew she had already spent years teaching me.

She and Abigail would be gone for a few more hours, giving me time to prepare a good meal for Ross, clean the kitchen, and then have time to deliver it to the greenhouse.

I added several logs to the wood-burning stove and carefully filled a pan with water. I began boiling the potatoes immediately. The roast beef was already cooked, and the green beans only needed to be thawed and warmed.

When I was finished, I put the hot food on a large plate, covered it with a dish towel, and placed it at the bottom of a cardboard box. I wrapped a few cookies in a separate towel and placed them on top.

I had little concern that anyone would stop me and inquire about the box on my way to the greenhouse, even though I had never carried a cardboard box there before. The greenhouse was my area of Preparation, and it seemed perfectly natural that people would think I was carrying seeds, small tools, or other supplies.

When everything was packed, I left the house through the back door and walked briskly to the greenhouse.

***

I found Ross in the utility closet, sleeping under a large wool blanket. I gently nudged his shoulder, but he barely moved. After setting the food on a nearby table, I tried to wake him again. This time, he began to stir.

"Ross, it's me, Hannah. I've brought you some food."

He must have been in a deep sleep. It took him several seconds to wake up enough that he could even focus his eyes and look at me. When he finally seemed coherent and aware of his surroundings, he smiled.

"Eat with me," he insisted. "I haven't shared a meal with anyone in so long, and I don't mean to be offensive, but you look like you need a good meal yourself."

I nodded. It had only been an hour since my massive egg sandwich, but my body had lacked proper nourishment for so long that I was ready to eat again. After unpacking the box, we sat on the floor and ate and talked like regular human beings. It was almost like we actually lived and enjoyed normal lives.

He talked about how good the food was, and I talked about my mother and what a gifted cook she was. He asked what she was doing this morning, and after I told him, he became strangely quiet, and I knew our conversation had strayed too close to unpleasant realities I desperately wanted to avoid.

He dropped his fork against the plate and looked away. "You have to know this is all so wrong."

"What's all wrong?" I muttered.

"Tying another human being to a tree and burning her to death. I can't believe something like that happened here."

The way he said it made it seem so different from how I had reasoned it all through in my mind. The words rattled around in my head like jagged glass, and all I could do was turn the conversation back on him.

"Like when you couldn't see how messed up your life was until bad things started happening?"

He seemed surprised that I'd said that. "Yeah, something like that. You know, sometimes we find ourselves in a place where we don't see things clearly. We justify, we rationalize, and we think things aren't really as bad as they are."

"Is that what you think I'm doing?"

"I think that's what both of us have done at certain times in our lives."

It was obvious that he wasn't going to push me any further than I was able to go at this point. So, I took the opportunity to learn more about who he was and why he was here. "Tell me more about your life and how you ended up here."

I listened as he told his story, this time in more detail. In some ways, his life sounded painfully similar to my own. He was raised in a Christian home, regularly attended church, and followed his faith as best he could as a young man living in difficult conditions.

"After my dad died, we lost the house, moved to a dangerous part of the city, and I started high school without the guidance of my father or having my former friends around. I started smoking weed during that time. It helped me forget my pain."

"I lost my dad, too. But it was after we came here. He died of cancer," I said.

"Hannah, I'm sorry."

He gently touched the top of my shoulder, and I felt safe and secure. It was what I imagined it would feel like if I had an older brother or a cousin to comfort me.

"Sometimes it takes a traumatic experience to wake a person up," he said gently. "Or perhaps someone from the outside letting you know just how off the mark a situation is."

He was again trying to ease me into a topic of conversation I didn't believe I was ready for. I suddenly felt very full, and my stomach was queasy. "I know things are not the way they're supposed to be here. I know what's happening is not the normal way of life. What you don't understand is that most of us here are trapped."

"Like I'm trapped?" He stood up and stretched his arms behind his head. "Do you think it would be ridiculous for me just to spend the rest of my life hiding in this greenhouse, never seeing my family or facing what I've done?"

"But isn't that why you ran away? So you wouldn't have to go back and face it?"

He shrugged. "I guess. But after thinking about it, I see how unrealistic that is and how wrong."

"But despite the terrible things that have happened here, there are good things about the Community. I have friends here.

My family is here," I said, trying to convince myself as well as Ross.

"There are good things about staying in the greenhouse, too. I'm safe, I'm warm, and I have food to eat."

"You're an adult. I'm not. You don't have a family counting on you to stay. I do."

He nodded. "You're right. You can't leave this place by yourself. You need help. As soon as I'm better, I'm going to leave. And when I'm strong enough, I'll be able to help you leave. That is, if you want my help."

The next breath I took seemed to hang in the air forever. "I don't know about that. Like I said, I'm not by myself. I have a family here."

"I know." He was more sympathetic to my indecision than I thought he would be. "It'll be a few more weeks before I'm ready to leave. I'm guessing by Easter, I'll be strong enough. Just think about what I've said."

I couldn't bring myself to answer and only slowly nodded. A thousand thoughts were swirling through my mind. What happened to Whitney, what was going on between Patrick and Alison, and Ross staying for a few more weeks before leaving was all too much to concentrate on. Suddenly, I thought how risky it was for him to stay in the greenhouse.

"I think you should stay in the cabins until you're ready to leave. I know you came to the greenhouse to find food, but now that I'm helping you, I can bring all the food you need to the cabins. It will be safer there."

"You're probably right. I'll go tonight after dark."

***

On a sunny Saturday afternoon in mid-March, just as the weather was improving and a hint of spring could be seen on everything from the growing maple trees to the meadowlarks flying against the deepening blue hues of the sky, the Community had its first gathering since Whitney's death. It was complete with frightening competitions, massive amounts of food, and the ever-watchful eyes of the elders.

Today's gathering, however, would have an event that would provide more distress than usual. The ax competition. Ax competitions only took place once every few months. The elders revered and respected nature, and we were not to take more trees than we needed or were able to replace.

This was the only competition the girls didn't participate in. And it was one of the few times I was thankful to be a female in the Community.

The ax competitions were done in pairs, so the men in the Community would learn to rely on one another and develop a sense of teamwork. As one young man held a log on a stump, the other would chop it in half. Then, they would switch places. The amount of trust – and fear that went along with holding a log in your hand while your partner chopped – was something I supposed only those going through it could understand.

The purpose was to cut the log as close to the center as possible. The elders would measure both sides to determine which team was the closest to splitting their logs through the center. All of this was fine and well, except that the logs became smaller and smaller as the competition progressed. Finally, the log being split did not have a circumference much wider than a twig.

"Take your places," Jonathon Alden announced.

All of the young men had already chosen their partners ahead of the competition, and they each took their positions behind a stump while the rest of the Community stood quietly in their designated spots. Patrick and Robbie McVeigh delivered logs of varying sizes to each team.

The young man with the ax was to concentrate on chopping the log precisely down the middle. The one who held the log was responsible for pulling his hands back in time if the chopper missed his target. Above all, they were to be brave and show no fear. Pulling their hands away too soon or displaying fear was worse than an uneven chop or completely missing.

Jonah McVeigh and Abner Coleman stood behind the last stump. Jonah, the son of Hayden and Elizabeth, was only mediocre with an ax. Abner, however, was one of the best wood splitters in the Community. When it came time to arrange marriage partners, everyone knew that getting a glowing report in the Community book for the ax competition put a young man in high standing.

Abigail was standing so close to me that her left shoulder blade pierced my ribs. "Abner's really good with an ax," Abigail whispered. "They should do well."

Abner held the log, which was not much larger than a medium-sized twig. Jonah lifted the ax above his head and bore down hard. Blood immediately splattered several feet beyond the stump. Abner didn't make a sound. He hadn't realized two of his fingers were missing until he looked down at the bloody stump.

He promptly passed out, and Ruth Anne Weber was immediately summoned.

# Chapter Sixteen

Now that Whitney was gone and the grievous sins that she had committed had been washed away with her death, we were told to forget about what had recently happened and to immerse ourselves in the Preparation. My mother said if Hayden McVeigh and Jonathan Alden said it was so, then it had to be.

I found that it helped to keep busy with our work. All the raw emotions I'd been feeling – fear, confusion, and anger – I pushed down deep inside of myself and covered the enormous grief with time spent in the Preparation.

Learning to sew, cook, and properly care for a home filled my days. I also allowed myself to look forward to the day I would be engaged and planning a wedding that would take place sometime in the autumn.

My greatest happiness was working in the greenhouse. Within a few weeks, we would begin planting the garden outside. I spent every hour I was allowed planting new seeds, carefully watering them, and coming up with my unique fertilizer combinations to make sure they grew as quickly as possible. Of course, all this meant that at least subconsciously, I'd made the decision not to leave with Ross.

That afternoon, as the four of us wandered into the fields to gather sticks, it didn't take long for the conversation to turn to Abner Coleman's severed fingers.

Abner's left-hand ring finger and pinky finger had almost completely been chopped off. Ruth Anne had sewn up the ends and wrapped the stubs in bandages. The elders then buried the ends of his chopped fingers in a small box in the Community cemetery. They believed they had to be buried just like the rest of the body so that God could reattach them on Resurrection Day.

"I believe God is powerful enough to reattach the fingers even if they disintegrated in a trash can somewhere," Katie said.

"It's not about whether God is powerful enough," Lynette insisted. "It's about following proper procedures and doing everything according to the Bible."

Alison shook her head. "And where exactly in the Bible does it say we have to bury people's fingers or God can't put them back on again?"

"It must be in there somewhere or the elders wouldn't do it," Lynette insisted.

"But what if it's not?" Alison said.

For some reason, all this talk about Abner's fingers made me angry, and I blurted out the first thing that came to my mind, "Abner's fingers got a better burial than Whitney's entire body."

Everyone looked at me like they couldn't believe I'd said that, but no one said anything. Not even Alison.

"We haven't gathered over there for a while," I said as I pointed to a small wooded area with an overgrown thicket next to it.

For the next thirty minutes, we filled both wheelbarrows with enough kindling to keep the Community fires burning for the next twenty-four hours.

Lynette carefully looked over both wheelbarrows, making sure all the sticks were the proper size. "Are we ready to go back?" she said.

"You and Katie take the wheelbarrows back. I need to talk to Alison," I said. "We'll only be a few minutes."

Katie looked at us strangely and then slowly turned and followed Lynette. Of course, she didn't understand what was going on and probably had a dozen questions. For some reason, a boldness was spilling out of me, and I was feeling strong enough to speak what was on my mind and ask the questions I needed answers to.

As soon as Katie and Lynette were gone, a deafening silence filled the spaces between Alison and me. I sat down next to her on a thick stump, trying to organize all the thoughts bouncing through my head.

"You've been seeing Patrick on a regular basis." I didn't look at her when I said it. I didn't want to overwhelm her and corner her into lying.

She walked away from me, and for a moment, I thought she would leave. When I finally got up and grabbed her arm, I could see into her deep brown eyes that everything I suspected was true. "Just admit it," I pleaded. "Too much has happened. Don't lie to me about this."

She loosened herself from my grip but didn't walk away. "I suppose there's no use hiding it from you anymore. I know you already know about me and Patrick."

I was surprised by how candidly she said the words. Now that we were past her confession, my head was swimming with a million questions. But the only thing at that moment managing to make it out of my mouth was, "Why? Why would you want to be involved with Patrick?"

She smiled softly, but it was an expression I'd never seen on her face before. She looked confused, even lost. It was a part of Alison I had never known. She took a breath and began explaining how she had come to begin a relationship with Patrick McVeigh.

"He's different when just the two of us are alone. And his wife is just miserable. I mean, I feel sorry for her that she can't have kids, but she takes it out on him and treats him terribly. Everyone thinks she's so sweet and wonderful. They don't know how she treats him when they're alone."

"I don't think either one is so sweet or wonderful. And you don't know how she treats him either. You're not there. You only know what he tells you. Besides, how do you know it's all her fault they can't have any kids?"

She was suddenly flustered and overlooked the fact that I had berated her and had practically accused Patrick of lying to her about what his wife did or didn't do.

"According to Ruth Anne, it's a problem with Celia, not Patrick."

"Okay, so what if it is? The guy is married. What kind of future are you going to have with a married man? What happens when you get engaged?"

"I'm not thinking about that right now. I'm just trying to survive each day as it comes."

I almost asked, what if the elders found out, but stopped, realizing how ridiculous that question was. Patrick was an elder for all practical purposes. I finally understood why she was involved with a man like Patrick. She needed a respite from the Preparation, the endless chores, the blazing sermons, and, above all, the death of Whitney. She needed to hide in the company of another human being, preferably someone of the opposite sex. Even though there was no romantic or physical involvement between me and Ross, I had done the same thing.

"Are you mad that I kept this from you?" she asked.

"No, I'm not mad. I've been keeping something from you, too. And I have to tell someone or I'll go crazy."

Alison leaned back and looked at me with genuine surprise. It even seemed to humor her that I, of all people, would have a secret I just had to tell or I'd go crazy. And I instantly knew that she thought my secret was just like hers.

"I knew it!" she cried before I could say anything. "I thought I saw someone in the greenhouse with you!"

My heart began pounding wildly. If Alison saw Ross, there was a chance that someone else had seen him as well. "You saw him? You saw a man in the greenhouse?"

"Was it one of the McVeigh boys?" she asked.

"No! Absolutely not!"

"Okay, I'm sorry. I'm just trying to figure out why there would be a guy in the greenhouse with you. I mean, I only saw him from a distance."

"A guy was living in the greenhouse, but it's not what you think."

She looked at me like she didn't really believe me. Then I explained everything: how I found Ross in the greenhouse, that he had a leg injury, and that I was helping him hide and bringing him food.

"He's staying at the cabins now," I said. "I thought it would be safer."

"This shocks me more than if you had a guy you were seeing, you know, a boyfriend."

"Why? I'm helping someone."

"You're defying the elders. You're giving away rationed food. You're consorting with someone of the opposite sex – someone outside of the Community. Should I go on?"

I'd hardly thought of anything besides the fact that I was helping a lonely, injured man get better. I was uncomfortable that she'd brought all these things to my attention.

"He says once he's better, he'll help us leave the Community if that's what we want."

Alison's mouth fell open and her eyes grew wide. For once, I had caught her off guard.

"You're running away from the Community?" she said, barely above a whisper. She sounded like she was impressed that I might consider such a thing.

"I didn't say that. I said that Ross offered."

"And why would he offer to help us? How did he get injured? And how did he get here? None of this makes sense."

"Okay, okay, that's too many questions for right now. Besides, I can't answer all of them, because I don't know the answers. I'm still trying to figure all of this out myself."

"So, you want to stay here... and get married... and become a Community wife?" Alison asked. Perhaps she was trying to help me find the answers.

"I don't know. I don't know what to think about anything anymore." I hesitated, then I told her what I'd been doing. "I've been reading the Bible, trying to find answers."

"We're not supposed to try to understand the Bible on our own," Alison said.

"And we're not supposed to have affairs with married men," I said.

"You could be in serious trouble trying to understand the Scriptures on your own."

"I can't stop or explain it, but something's drawing me toward the Bible. It's interesting."

She seemed perplexed. Anything we weren't supposed to do, good or bad, caught Alison's attention.

"What's interesting about it?"

"God is interesting," I said.

She tilted her head and looked at me like she wasn't sure what I meant by that. "We need to get back," she said.

If she didn't want to talk about God, that was fine. But I needed to settle things about Ross. "You're not going to tell anyone about Ross, are you?"

She smiled. "No, I won't tell. And you won't tell anyone about Patrick, right?"

We both agreed.

## Counselor

"Did you feel better after telling Alison about Ross?" the counselor asks, looking like she already knows the answer.

"No. I thought I would, but I didn't."

"Why didn't you feel better?"

There's anger in my voice when I say, "Because it didn't change anything! In some ways, it made things worse." Anticipating her next question, I say, "The more people who knew he was there, the greater the chance the elders would find out. And I was terrified of what might happen if they did."

She's quiet for several seconds before leaning toward me. "Maybe it should have made you feel better. But I suspect very little would have eased your pain and confusion. You were in denial about Whitney's death. Your mind was protecting you by becoming occupied with other things."

"It just made everything more complicated – and riskier." I sat up straight and tall in the plush leather seat. "I'm not sure I made the right decision telling Alison when I did. But I have no doubt I made the right decision helping Ross."

She nods. "Why was it the right decision?"

"Even though I didn't see it at the time, I believe it was God's way of making me stronger. I could have shied away from that challenge. I could have turned him in or at least ignored him. But by taking that incredible risk of helping him, God was using that to ultimately set me free."

# Chapter Seventeen

After the initial shock of Whitney's death subsided into mind-numbing reality, the days that followed were filled with an unexplainable darkness. I thought of Whitney, and my chest hurt. If I thought about Ross, my nerves would tighten, and my heart would race. My mother saw the tension in my face and heard the fear in my voice.

She offered me the herbal remedies that Jada Brewer cooked up for soothing nerves and curing anxiety. The other women in the Community drank the herbal teas like liquid candy. But it caused my stomach to cramp, and I couldn't keep it down.

"In a few months, you'll be engaged and planning your wedding," my mother said in a choppy and uneven voice. "There will be dresses to choose from, a dinner menu to plan, and a new house to decorate. Everything that has you upset now will fade into the background." That was her final remedy to make me feel better.

She wouldn't look at me when she said it. Even she knew it was ridiculous to think a fancy dress and a dinner menu would make me forget the smell of Whitney's burning flesh. Still, she wouldn't stop talking.

All evening long, while cooking dinner and then helping Abigail get ready for bed, she talked about stitching handmade lace, cooking a feast for the reception, and the delicate flowers I would grow for my wedding. After a while, I tuned her out and just let her talk. It was her way of coping, I suppose.

When I woke up the next day, her words had melted away like the morning frost. The house was so cold. We hadn't anticipated a deep freeze in March and weren't allowed enough wood to keep the stove hot enough to warm the entire house.

As soon as I was dressed and had eaten my breakfast, I actually looked forward to leaving and beginning the morning's Preparation lessons. I knew before I arrived that an elder's house would be warmer than ours.

I met Lynette, Katie, and Alison behind the general store, and we walked the rest of the way together to Ruth Anne's home. We were coming upon the part of the Preparation that we believed would be the most enjoyable yet made us the most nervous.

Ruth Anne taught young girls coming of age in the Community how to be married. This included how to act, talk, and dress to be a good Community wife. From what the girls who were already married had told us in hushed conversations, sex was also discussed.

"I'm so nervous," Lynette said.

"There's nothing to be nervous about," Alison replied. "This is the easiest part of the Preparation."

"But it's the most embarrassing," Katie said.

"Because Ruth Anne talks about sex?" Alison said sarcastically. "I probably know more about sex than Ruth Anne does."

I didn't say a word when she said that. I didn't want to know anything more about Alison and Patrick than I already did.

When Lynette inquired exactly what and how Alison knew about sex, Alison had an answer that satisfied the question without giving away her terrible secret.

"The Colorado public schools give pretty explicit information these days about sex. You do know I went to a regular school until I was fifteen?"

That was the end of that conversation, but we were about to begin another one of the same type when Ruth Anne opened her front door and invited us inside. The four of us sat on a large sofa covered with thick blankets and plush pillows.

Ruth Anne pulled the matching recliner out toward the middle of the room to face us as she talked. We waited for several other girls to arrive and take their places on chairs arranged near the sofa.

Ruth Anne had given us a written quiz that asked several questions concerning sexuality during our first time together. We ate buttered popcorn and chocolate bars that had obviously been bought from the outside to make us feel more comfortable as we filled out embarrassing questions about our bodies, what we knew about a man's body, and what happened when those two bodies got together.

Ruth Anne sat down and casually crossed her legs. "After reading everything you've written, I've decided upon a good place to start."

She gave a brief lesson on male and female body parts, how babies were made, and then told us that we were expected to make as many of them as possible. She then spent the remainder of the time telling us exactly how a good wife in the Community was to treat her husband.

"You must be faithful, obedient, and respectful at all times... doing whatever he requests," she stated plainly.

I imagined Timothy Lane, tall and muscular, coming home from his profession in the Community while Gretchen painstakingly prepared meals over a stove as hot as hellfire. I could see Timothy complaining and sending her back to the fire to redo whatever dish she had prepared that evening.

"You must never question your husband's authority! You must cater to his every whim," she said.

Then I imagined the face of Patrick McVeigh, as pale as November snow. He was another woman's husband. Why would I think of him? Probably because I knew he was "with" Alison and was at least attempting to be with several other young, single girls as well.

Of course, Celia was bitter and unhappy all the time. But she could never question or accuse him, even when he was committing such terrible sins.

"And if he instructs you to do so, you will wear items such as these."

I gasped for breath when she opened a small box and pulled out a negligee. I wasn't sure what it was at first. There were pieces of sheer black lace and thin ribbon intricately connected with red bows. I would not have known what it was except for the bra at the top of the garment.

"And you will not complain... about anything."

No wonder nearly all the married women in the Community were always angry. I was thankful that my mother had remained a widow after my father passed away. I slowly looked around at my sisters in suffering.

Katie and Lynette appeared as bewildered as I'm sure I did. Alison looked stoic and resolved to whatever was expected of us. None of this surprised her, but even Alison didn't look happy about it.

While Ruth Anne neatly folded the lacy, stringy undergarment back into the small box, I decided at that moment that I didn't ever want to be a Community wife. The most beautiful wedding dress in the world and the most delicious dinner menu could never make up for the years of suffering and misery I was convinced would follow.

***

When it was time to gather wood, I told the others to follow me into an area that I knew was especially thick with canopies full of vines that would hide us even from the birds flying overhead. Finding the proper-sized kindling would be easier in this area, and it would also give us more privacy.

"Why did you bring us to this part of the woods?" Lynette complained. "I'm going to get scratched to pieces."

"I have to talk to you," I said firmly. I was afraid for a moment that I shouldn't tell them about Ross. I loved Lynette and Katie and knew they wouldn't purposely tell anyone. But they weren't as strong as Alison, and I was afraid they would somehow let it slip out unintentionally.

"Talk about what?" Katie asked.

There was still time to lie. I could make up almost anything regarding what I wanted to "talk about." But I didn't. Telling the others would force me to make some serious decisions I wasn't sure I was ready to make.

"Follow me," I said. I continued deeper into the woods to a spot I knew where several trees had fallen during the last storm. I was swerving around thickets of thorns, ducking under thick, low branches. I looked back only once, and seeing they were all still following me, I continued until coming to the place where we could sit on the logs instead of standing.

"Okay, I've got something really important to tell all of you."

"Let me guess!" Katie said after finally catching her breath. "The elders have already found a husband for you. I know they sometimes do that if they see an obvious match before the Preparation is over."

I looked up at the rising moon, ashen gray and vaporous. It wasn't going to be a full moon, but it was going to be bright once it rose completely into the night sky.

"No. I'm not engaged. But what I have to tell you is about a man." Both sets of eyes across from me widened, and I couldn't help but let them lead themselves on just a little before telling them about Ross.

"Are you going out with someone before the elders have picked someone for you?" Lynette asked. Lynette had lived with members of the Community her entire life. The thought of actually dating, spending time alone with the opposite sex, or even picking her own husband was something she had never even thought was a possibility.

"No," I finally said. "I'm not involved with any man, at least not in a romantic way."

I had Katie and Lynette's full attention.

"Listen carefully, and don't say anything until I'm done explaining."

They both eagerly nodded.

"Several weeks ago, while working in the greenhouse, I discovered a man hiding in the back near the utility closet."

Both girls gasped but followed my instructions and didn't say a word. Alison remained uncharacteristically quiet as well.

"He was injured with a leg wound and was staying in the greenhouse trying to recuperate when I found him. I don't know all the details. He isn't comfortable talking about it, but he was shot in the leg."

There was more gasping, widening of eyes, and leaning forward so they wouldn't miss a single word of what I would say next.

"His name is Ross Sullivan, and he's a Black man."

The looks on their faces suddenly changed from anticipation to confusion. Both Katie and I had had very few interactions with African Americans our entire lives. I don't think Lynette had ever even seen a Black person.

"Since he's better, he's staying at the back cabin. In a week or so, he should be well enough to leave."

"So there were never any witches. It was Ross," Katie interrupted, finally putting it all together.

"That's right," I said. "Now, listen carefully."

I took a deep breath before revealing the final part. For some reason, I hadn't been that frightened to tell them about Ross. But now I was very reluctant to go on, probably because everything I had told them had already passed or only involved Ross. What came next involved each one of us and our futures.

"Ross said when he's strong enough to leave, he'll help the rest of us leave, too. If that's what we want."

I expected an immediate reaction and was surprised when I didn't get one. The last words I spoke seemed to hang in the air above us, waiting to be accepted or repudiated. I looked up to see if they were hanging above my head, but there was nothing except swift-moving clouds lingering above a tangle of branches.

Finally, Lynette began to process what she'd just heard, and the negative reaction I had initially anticipated began to take shape. It started with shaking her head in disbelief that such a thing as leaving with a stranger had even been suggested.

"All of this is crazy talk," she said stiffly.

Katie, however, was more practical. "Even if we would consider leaving, where would we go? Our families are all here."

I couldn't answer that question, so I asked one I thought that she wouldn't be able to answer, either. "If you had a chance to leave the Community, would you?"

Her expression and sudden change in body posture told me I'd completely caught her off guard. "Why would I want to leave the Community?" She quickly looked around, afraid that even here, in the middle of the deepest part of the woods, someone might be listening to our conversation.

Alison stood up and leaned forward. "Don't tell me that thought has never crossed your mind."

"Not really," Katie said, sounding like she meant it. "Because it's not a possibility."

"None of us should be talking about things like this!" Lynette cried, rising to her feet.

"But it is a possibility," I insisted.

"This man, Ross, how is he living and eating and getting medicine for his wound?" Lynette asked.

"From me. I've been helping him."

My admission of complicity had stunned Lynette into silence. A soft breeze was swirling into the thicket, bringing in the cold night air.

"Even if you don't want any part of this, you've all got to promise not to tell a soul. Not anyone."

Lynette and Katie looked at each other for approval and then slowly nodded and muttered their promises.

"No matter how bad things get, we can't tell a soul that Ross is living in the cabins," I insisted. "It won't help anyone, especially us, so don't tell anyone!"

We squeezed our hands together so tightly that my fingers hurt, each swearing we wouldn't tell about Ross.

# Chapter Eighteen

G retchen was almost six months pregnant and rarely came to the greenhouse anymore. Between taking care of her two small children and preparing for the birth of her third child, she had neither the time nor the energy for weeding, watering, and preparing fertilizer.

I'd been in training for over two months and, before that, had spent years working with my mother in the substantial garden behind our home. I was more than capable of running the greenhouse on my own, and the fact that she stayed away so much proved that she trusted me.

I watered the spinach and the lettuce. I looked at the cabbage twice before deciding it didn't need fertilizer today. I measured the carrots with my fingers and immediately knew they needed thinning.

Working in the greenhouse was a gift from God that I now gave thanks for regularly. It made me appreciate things like having enough food, a warm house, and a purpose that made me want to get out of bed every morning.

I took a small bag of fertilizer and headed toward the tomato plants, glancing occasionally at the utility closet where Ross had stayed. I knew I needed to clean out the inside of the closet before Gretchen or anyone else would happen to go inside. There were old clothes, bloody bandages, and dirty plates that would give away the fact that someone had been staying there.

I put on a thin pair of gloves and began mixing the fertilizer. Using a large bucket, I created my own recipe with manure from the animal pens, leftover coffee grinds, and a mix of herbs. I sprinkled it all into the bucket.

Fear and hope swirled in my head, thoughts as countless as the granules of herbs between my fingers. And the secrets tangled between them made it nearly impossible for me to organize my thoughts rationally. Ross living in the cabin, Alison with Patrick, and the fear and desperation that hung as thick as fog over the Community since Whitney's death all created a cloud of confusion in my brain.

A loud knock at the greenhouse door caused me to jolt up from the bucket I'd been leaning over. Alison knocked on the main door again, stuck her head inside, and then called for me to come out into the cold. I don't think Alison had ever been to the greenhouse to see me. I knew immediately something wasn't right, and any sense of tranquility I had left drained from my soul as quickly as the heat poured out of the greenhouse behind me.

"What's going on?" I asked.

Her dark eyes flickered as she quickly looked in all directions to make sure no one had seen her come to the greenhouse. "Can I come inside? I have to show you something." She was trying to talk in a loud whisper and sounded strange.

I hurried toward the door as a gust of wind suddenly swept around Alison's body and caught me by surprise. This wind was strong and still incredibly cold for March. "Get in here before someone sees you. What is it? I'm in the middle of doing my work."

She grabbed my hand and pulled me to the innermost part of the greenhouse, stopping between a row of gangly tomato plants and clusters of spinach. She reached into the deepest pocket of her overalls and pulled out a crumpled newspaper. Alison snapped open the newspaper, the words screaming beneath my face. The headline read:

*Ross Sullivan Wanted for the Murder of Elderly Woman in Cheyenne, Wyoming*

It felt like a lightning bolt had just raced through my brain. "What is this?"

"Since you obviously don't want to read it, I'll read it for you."

Before she could say anything else, I grabbed the paper and read the article. I had to convince myself that I had at least some control over what was a terrible revelation. My eyes quickly scanned the article, picking up words and phrases as my brain tried to reassemble the information.

*... convenience store robbed... man beaten... $400 in cash stolen ... man's wife shot at point-blank range... woman died instantly...*

*Ross Sullivan and another unidentified accomplice are wanted in connection with the murder after being denied bail and escaping custody.*

There was a scratchy picture of Ross next to the article. I dropped the newspaper on the ground. Alison snatched it as I walked toward the door.

"Where are you going?" Alison said.

"To talk to Ross, I have to find out the truth."

Alison leaned toward me and shook the newspaper in my direction. "You already know the truth."

"No. I know what some reporter somewhere has decided is the truth. I have to find out if it really is."

I didn't look back again to see if she was still shaking the paper or getting ready to tell me that it was more than one reporter's opinion. He was on the run from the police. He had been arrested, denied bail, and then escaped when being transported back to the jail. But I wouldn't let myself think about that until I had a chance to talk to him.

I walked as quickly as I could without running. I would stop at home first and put on a warmer coat. I would hide some food in my pockets and then make my way to the cabin. As soon as I got home, it was obvious I wasn't going to make it to the cabin, at least not tonight.

***

My mother was in the kitchen, standing over a huge pot that was boiling furiously on the stove. "I need you to deliver food and medicine for me tonight."

I looked around the kitchen. She was filling baskets with broiled beef, vegetables, desserts, and herbal remedies that Jada Brewer had brought over. Something had been building in the Community during the days since Whitney's death. I had sensed it almost immediately. But I'd been able to hide from it in the greenhouse and in my time spent with Ross.

Spending even a small amount of time with someone who wasn't from the Community provided me with emotional support that the others didn't have.

I could see clearly that fear, grief, and despair had grown stronger each day that Whitney lay in her shallow grave behind the Crouse home. This unimaginable thing had taken root inside each member of the Community. Some were stronger than others, able to struggle through it and somehow rise above it to keep from drowning in each breath.

For those who weren't as strong, it was now growing inexplicably and strangling their hearts and minds. Emotional despair and mental illness were now epidemic in the Community.

My mother was cooking meals for several families in the Community who were having "troubles," as it was now called. It would be up to Lynette and me to deliver the meals to each home. Most of the houses we came to were quiet and dark. Fear had suffocated each home and muted their voices, dimmed the lanterns, and caused each inhabitant to lie lethargically about the house.

While my mother was feverishly cooking succulent roasts and hearty beef stews, Jada Brewer was busy preparing dried chamomile and valerian. At just the precise time, she would remove the tray, let the flowers cool, and later add other ingredients such as catnip, lavender, and rosemary. Taking delicate paper tea bags, she would painstakingly fill each one with just the right amount and properly seal it.

When herbal remedies weren't enough, alcohol was the medication of choice. Some alcohol was brought in from the outside, and the rest was crudely made by allowing sugar, yeast, and allotted portions of orange juice to ferment. Alcohol had always been allowed in the Community, especially for men, when consumed in limited amounts.

Now, the elders turned a blind eye to the excessive drinking that was occurring among men and women alike. Considering the current condition of most of us in the Community, the drinking of alcohol filtered down to teenagers and children as well.

Finally, two days later, after the Community had stuffed themselves with food, alcohol, and herbal remedies and had found what they believed was the answer to their pain, I was able to slip away.

# Chapter Nineteen

I packed some leftover food and quietly left the house before the sun rose on a windy Thursday morning. As I stood on our front steps, scanning the Community as far as I could see in every direction, I waited to hear if I'd woken my mother.

If she knew I was leaving, she would ask why I was going out so early. But she was exhausted from spending every waking hour during the last few days cooking for families in the Community.

I peered into the blackness of the main road, food for Ross tucked in the inside of my coat. If by chance I was stopped and questioned, I'd already decided I'd say I was going to the woods for some wild herbs to mix into fertilizer for the greenhouse.

As far as the food was concerned, I'd initially thought I'd say it was my breakfast. But there was too much there. I figured it would be better to say I was going to give it to one of the families my mother had cooked for. No matter what they asked me or when I got stopped, everything was taken care of.

But I didn't get stopped.

With each step, I stretched an imaginary rubber band between myself and the Community that I feared could snap at any moment. The wind seemed more than willing to pull me farther away, into the meadow, and toward the cabins.

Ross had increasingly become my confidant, my anchor in the raging sea of the uncertainty that was my life. I feared losing the only real friendship I had established with someone from the outside world since I was in the second grade. Even the death of a friend didn't seem as bad as this possibility. There were some things worse than even death.

I stood in front of the cabin door for several seconds before knocking. I could still go back. I could forget I'd ever met Ross and go home and concentrate on finishing the Preparation, finding a husband, and forgetting everything that had happened during the last month. While my brain was deciding, my hand instinctively reached up and knocked.

"Come in." His voice was surprisingly cheerful and inviting.

But the silence inside was more frightening than the gusts of wind that continued to swirl on the outside. If he really was a murderer and I confronted him, what would stop him from killing me? I didn't think he had a weapon, but I couldn't be sure. He was larger than me but injured. As I concluded that his injured leg would make us both a pretty even match, he called my name.

"Hannah, I'm over here, by the window."

As he was looking out the window, I watched him from behind. His hair was starting to get long now. It was wiry and unruly, but it looked like he had washed it and tried to pat it down with layers of water and soap. His clothes were still ragged and dirty, but he was clean and moving around without much of a limp. I stood just beyond the door, my feet like stuck clay.

"Is something wrong?" he asked.

I immediately backed away, wanting to put more distance between us before I told him what I knew.

"I found out something about you a few days ago."

His face immediately drooped as if a heavy weight had been attached to it. "Have you read about me in a newspaper?"

"How did you know?" I said nervously.

It looked like he tried to smile, but the corners of his mouth wouldn't cooperate. "You told me there weren't any phones, TVs, or computers in the Community, and that new people rarely came in. I figured eventually you'd see a newspaper."

"Is it true? Did you kill an old woman?" I suddenly felt vulnerable and looked to see how much distance was between myself and the door.

"No. I didn't kill her." He looked me in the eye when he said it, sounding so calm. He was either the best liar in the world or it was the truth.

Suddenly, without any warning, he began to cry. He pulled out a chair and sat down. I watched anxiously as he buried his face in his hands and wept. When he finally caught his breath and looked up at me again, he tearfully explained what had happened.

"I was tired of not finding a job, of every opportunity being denied me."

I pulled out another chair and sat down next to him.

"My mother was having trouble paying the rent. I was coming down from the drugs, and my girlfriend was tired of waiting around for me to get my life together." He leaned down to momentarily let his head rest in his hands, knots of wiry hair getting tangled in his fingers.

I suddenly felt overwhelming compassion for him. Before I knew it, my hand was lightly touching his shoulder, and I'd forgotten all about being afraid of him.

"We decided to rob a convenience store on the south end of Cheyenne. The place had limited surveillance and was run by a couple of old people. We thought it would be easy money, and no one would put up a fight."

He then explained how their simple plan spiraled out of control. "The old couple was so feisty. They put up more of a fight than we figured they would. While the old lady fought for the phone with the guy I was with, the old man tried to take hold of my gun."

He stopped for a second, shaking his head. He seemed surprised when listening to the events of his own story. "I hit the old man with the end of my gun. The other guy who was with me... shot the old guy's wife."

We were quiet for several seconds while the wind picked up again outside. I was glad it was howling so loudly. It was able to fill the empty spaces between us.

"We were arrested only hours after it happened. Because of overcrowding, they were sending us to the Rawlins, Wyoming Correctional Facility. When they were transporting us, I saw my chance to get the key. I thought we were going to get away without any trouble. And we almost did. Then, one of the officers shot me in the leg. I just kept running and realized later that the bullet skimmed through the top of my thigh."

He suddenly looked up and grabbed my arm. I couldn't have gotten away from him if I'd wanted to. But I was so immersed in his story that I'd forgotten all about my fear.

"I did hit the old man. I couldn't bring myself to shoot him, so I hit him with the end of the gun so I could get away. I'm not proud of myself. I just wanted to get out of there." He let go of my arm and looked down at his hands after he said it. "I didn't shoot the old woman. I promise to God in heaven, I didn't shoot her."

His eyes were red and his skin had turned ash gray. But I believed him. I had rarely sensed such sincerity or heartfelt remorse in my entire life.

"Then why did you run away? Why didn't you stay and tell them you were innocent?"

"Because I wasn't innocent, not completely. I did hit the man and robbed the couple. I did enough to warrant jail time."

"What happened to the other guy you were with?"

"I don't know. I'm assuming they caught him."

I leaned back in the stiff wooden chair and tried to absorb everything he'd just told me. Our lives, our situations, and our individual culpability were completely different, yet at that moment, I had never felt so connected to another human being in my entire life.

We were both trapped, each of us facing potentially life-or-death circumstances, and both of us were terrified out of our minds. We were both staring at one another in this isolated cabin in the middle of the Wyoming winter, wondering if we would ever find the way out of the situations we were in.

Looking at him so closely frightened me. It wasn't because I didn't believe him. It scared me to look so deeply into his eyes. The desperation and the uncertainty, it was all too familiar. We were close enough that I could feel it with each breath he took.

"Your leg is almost healed now. You need to leave as soon as possible," I said softly.

"So you don't believe me?"

"I do, but knowing you're on the run for murder only complicates matters. My life is difficult enough."

He must have sensed what I was thinking, or perhaps he'd been thinking it himself all along. Either way, I could see it in his face that he, too, was seeing the parallels in both our lives.

He reached for my shoulders and squeezed. "You know you're living in a cult, a dangerous, murderous cult. You have to get out. We have to help each other."

I could barely get the words out. "Even if you didn't kill that woman, you were involved with someone who did!"

"And you're not involved with people who killed another innocent human being?" He said it barely above a whisper, but every painful word stuck in my brain. My face felt like it was on fire. "It's not the same thing," I insisted.

He shook his head and then looked away. "People are dead. It's the same thing to them."

I pulled myself free of his grasp and flew out of the chair so fast it almost fell over. "No... no... it's not the same thing."

I grabbed the door handle, stopped, and turned around. I took the food I had brought and quickly set it on the table. "I'll bring you more food in a few days. You'll be well enough to leave then."

"Bring enough for yourself, too. We'll leave together."

I opened the door and left without looking back.

***

I had been running faster than I'd ever run in my life. The wind had died down, and the air had warmed slightly since I'd come to the cabin. This improvement in weather enabled me to run longer and breathe easier. I slowed down when I saw the roofs of the houses peaking up beyond the bushes.

I entered the Community on the east side, knowing I'd have to pass by two rows of houses, the main road, and then make my way past another row of houses until I came to ours. I immediately regretted taking this route when I saw Steve Flowers repairing a window in his house.

He only turned and looked at me once, but I could tell by his expression that he was uncomfortable with my presence, and he wanted to ask why I was walking through his yard, coming from the middle of nowhere.

But he lifted the small hammer and went about his business of pounding nails into a windowsill that had cracked under the strain of a harsh winter. He had enough to worry about with Alison. I was almost certain he would turn the other way, even if he knew I was doing something inappropriate.

After passing the next row of houses, I thought I would blend in easily and not be questioned. The Community Hall and the general store were on the main road, and there could be a dozen reasons why I'd be in this area. It was mid-morning now, and I could see several people going about their business.

"Hannah!"

The sound of his voice caused me to abruptly stop and turn to face him like a soldier under command. Hayden McVeigh was standing on his front porch holding a mug of coffee. I could see the steam rising through the morning air and circling under his square chin.

"Come here, girl."

I thought of the punishments that I had recently endured. During the last three months, I had gone through a wind cleansing and had my hand stabbed with a sewing needle. What else could they do to me? Then, the face of Whitney Crouse, as beautiful as an antique doll, flashed before my eyes.

"Where have you been?" he demanded.

"Searching for wild mint to put into my fertilizer mix," I said evenly.

"Did you find any?" He held the coffee under his chin and let the steam warm his face.

"No, sir, I didn't."

He finally took a sip while looking out toward the north meadow. "Of course, you didn't. Wild mint only grows in the fields to the west. Now, you best be on your way."

I knew he was watching me as I walked the rest of the way home. I could feel the cold stare of his eyes on the back of my head. I didn't dare look back, though. I was certain there was enough power in those eyes to pull me back to him at will, without even blinking.

I concentrated on each step, making sure to walk straight and tall. And somehow, by the mercy of a God who was becoming more real to me with each passing day, I made it back to the house without my legs collapsing beneath me.

# Chapter Twenty

During the next few days, I spent every spare moment scouring the Bible, reading and studying dozens of chapters. Each verse was like a piece of a puzzle. When I found different sections that seemed to fit together and explain what other passages meant, it was like fitting one more piece in place. In the end, I believed this giant face of God would emerge.

I was so immersed in reading Scripture that I became careless when hiding it from my mother. I would forget to close my door completely or not pull up the covers when she would walk by. I shouldn't have been surprised when she suddenly came into my room with a stack of folded laundry and proceeded to drop it all when she saw I was reading the Bible.

"Haven't you been in enough trouble?" she said.

"That's exactly right. That's why I want to find out who Christ is, and reading His Word is the logical way to do it."

"Following the elders' rules will help you find out what knowing Christ is all about," my mother insisted.

"Following God is not about rules and constant fear of punishment," I said.

"*The fear of the Lord is the beginning of wisdom*," my mother said.

"*Perfect love casteth out fear*," I said, holding out the Bible. If only she'd read it on her own, really read it, I just knew she'd figure this out for herself.

"But we're not perfect, are we?" she countered.

"I don't think that verse is talking about us being perfect, at least not by ourselves, outside of Christ."

She picked up the laundry off the floor, quickly refolded it, and set it on my dresser. Before leaving, she went to my window and shut the curtains. "If you insist on doing this, please be careful."

"I will," I said excitedly.

The more I read and prayed, the more I forced myself not to listen whenever Hayden or Jonathon breathed fire over the pulpit. I would lose myself in my thoughts. I would recite the few Scriptures I'd memorized over and over again.

Sometimes, when their voices were too loud to drown out, I would find an object on the wall, anything I could stare at and fix my gaze on. It had to be something close to where the men were standing so no one would notice I wasn't looking at them and not paying attention. Again, I would concentrate and recite the verses in my head.

With only a small candle for light in my bedroom late in the evening, I would pore over the pages of my mother's Bible. The more I understood what real faith and genuine Christianity were all about, the more convinced I became that it wasn't happening in the Community. And the more terrified I became. But despite my terror, there was peace and hope I could sense pulling me toward God.

During this time, thoughts of actually leaving the Community began to take root in my mind. Listening to Hayden and Jonathon hadn't caused me to want to leave. Even watching Whitney burn to death had only told me to stay. But reading this Bible night after night planted seeds of leaving in my brain. Fear told me to stay. Hope told me to go. And I was finally beginning to understand which voice was telling the truth.

****

The rain poured in sheets across our front window. Although there would be spurts of snow on and off for the next few weeks, for the most part, winter in Wyoming was over. What started only a few minutes earlier as a few drops along the windowpane quickly escalated into a tirade of streaming water.

The dirt road in front of our house filled quickly with tiny ravines, like miniature muddy rivers flowing through the Community. I sat at the window for several minutes, staring into the downpour. I felt safe, trapped inside by walls of freezing March rain.

My mother was scurrying back and forth behind me, straightening the quilts on the sofa and chairs, dusting the coffee table, and then running back to the kitchen every few minutes to check the chicken in the oven. I heard the oven door open and shut.

"It's not going to get done in time," she said nervously. Then the door next to the oven opened, and I could hear several logs thrown on the fire. After shutting the door, her frantic footsteps beat across the wooden floor. "Is your bedroom clean?"

Mesmerized by the falling rain, I didn't bother to turn around. "I'll do it in a little bit."

"Please, do it now, and change clothes. You know we're having the McVeighs for dinner in less than an hour." She hurried back into the kitchen, opened and closed several cabinets, and then called back into the living room. "And make sure Abigail wears her blue and white dress."

She was truly frightened at the prospect of doing anything that would be perceived as even the least bit wrong while the McVeighs were in our home. If I had allowed myself to dwell on the fact for more than a few seconds that the head elder and his wife were coming for dinner, I might have fallen into a state of terror as well. But I was still so wrapped up in so many other emotions that terror had taken a backseat, at least for the time being.

Before she could ask me again, I retreated to my bedroom, but I didn't immediately get to work cleaning. Instead, I pulled the Bible from the dresser drawer, sat cross-legged on the bed, and reread my favorite verses. I had been reading long enough that I now had verses I returned to with great regularity.

I had three verses that I had written down on a small piece of paper, arranging them in the order they appeared in Scripture.

*And ye shall seek me, and find me, when ye shall search for me with all your heart.*   Jeremiah 29:13

*I love them that love me; and those that seek me early shall find me.*   Proverbs 8:17

*Ask, and it shall be given you; seek, and ye shall find; knock, and it shall be opened unto you: for every one that asketh receiveth; and he that seeketh findeth; and to him that knocketh it shall be opened.*    Matthew 7:7,8

I read these verses over and over, breathing in each word like oxygen for my soul. Abigail opened the door and stuck her head inside. "I'm supposed to check on you and see if you're about finished." She looked around the room and made a silly face. "It doesn't look like you've even started."

"Come here," I said, patting the bed next to where I was sitting. Abigail shut the door and crawled onto the bed next to me.

I slowly read my favorite verses to her. We were on a forbidden adventure, exploring magnificent things we had been warned not to see. She listened attentively as I explained the meaning as best I could.

"Those are pretty words," she said. "Almost like poetry."

I closed the Bible and returned it to its hiding place. "Will you help me get things cleaned up before I get into trouble?"

"Sure," she said with a smile.

***

Hayden and Elizabeth McVeigh showed up at our front door at six sharp, dressed in their finest attire. I had only seen Elizabeth wearing more jewelry and brighter colors during her oldest daughter's wedding.

"It's so nice to see you both. Please come in," my mother said the instant she opened the door.

Elizabeth nodded and smiled. Elizabeth's smile was the strangest thing I'd ever seen on a human face. Only the corners of her mouth moved while the rest of her face remained frozen as if it were etched in granite.

Of course, Hayden rarely smiled, so his expression never seemed to change. I think I'd caught him smiling on two separate occasions, but both had been from a distance, and it had been difficult to tell if his face had looked any different.

Abigail and I were perched on the sofa exactly where and how our mother had told us to sit, arranged like dolls on a shelf. When Elizabeth saw us, she smiled slightly again, letting my mother know that she was pleased with how we were dressed and arranged.

After my mother had invited them inside, Hayden headed straight for the solitary chair in the corner. Elizabeth, however, took a semi-circular path around the living room before sitting next to Abigail on the sofa. It was her way, I suppose, of examining our housekeeping abilities.

"Let's sit down and visit for a bit. Dinner will be ready in about ten minutes," my mother said.

My mother had orchestrated everything down to the last excruciating detail. This included where we each sat, topics to discuss, and exactly when the dinner would be ready. She must have thought that ten minutes was an adequate amount of time to talk before eating.

Ten minutes wasn't long at all if you were with people you enjoyed spending time with. I don't think she realized the agonizing eternity ten minutes was about to become with Hayden and Elizabeth McVeigh.

After my mother's list of conversation topics had been exhausted in only a few minutes, Elizabeth commented on how well my mother kept house, the lack of dust on the tables, and the scent of pine that permeated the front room.

Before my mother had finished eagerly thanking Elizabeth for her comment, Hayden took off on a mini-sermon about how cleanliness was next to godliness. I would find out later that there wasn't a verse in the Bible that said that. But his exhortation regarding scrubbing the flesh, the mind, and the soul lasted until the timer beeped in the kitchen, indicating that the chicken was ready.

"It's time to eat," my mother announced eagerly. She led each of us to our assigned places at the table.

While passing the dish of green beans, I purposely opened my hand so the scar on my palm could clearly be seen. But neither of the McVeighs seemed very interested in me this evening. Their focus was entirely on Abigail. They watched her attentively whenever she said anything, even something as insignificant as, "Please pass the chicken." And this concerned me.

Elizabeth seemed to be paying extra attention to my little sister. It was almost as if Abigail was auditioning for an important role she hadn't a clue she might possibly play.

"How is your schoolwork coming along?" Elizabeth asked.

"I'm doing well. I've already memorized my multiplication tables," Abigail said proudly. "Long division is proving more difficult, but I'm sure I'll get it down."

Elizabeth smiled with satisfaction, and again, the upper half of her face refused to move. Her gray eyes were frozen in their sockets, like a doll's eyes that were permanently tied together... left, right... up and back down again.

My mother had arranged ahead of time for Abigail to serve dessert. She brought the large chocolate cake to the table and set it between Elizabeth and Hayden. With a white bone china knife and matching cake server, Abigail elegantly cut and served the cake exactly the way my mother had instructed her.

My mother was undoubtedly the best baker in the Community, and this chocolate cake, topped with fresh fruit that had been brought into the general store just a day earlier, looked like it belonged in a gourmet bakery.

In her sweet, little girl voice, she asked if they wanted home-made vanilla ice cream. Both agreed, and Abigail served the ice cream as well.

It wasn't until after the dinner and much thought that I realized what my mother was doing. She was showcasing Abigail as potential wife material for Hayden and Elizabeth's eleven-year-old son.

Jonah McVeigh was a handsome blonde boy of eleven. He was quiet, well-behaved, and one of the more likable of the McVeigh children. There was not an elder's son in the appropriate age range for her to have had that option with me.

I hated that Abigail was being paraded around like a show animal on display. I had no idea, however, what was coming next. If I had, I might have insisted that Ross help us escape immediately and would have taken Abigail with us.

While my mother, Abigail, and I were washing the dinner dishes, Hayden and Elizabeth were in the living room with their heads together for several minutes. I could hear an occasional word and an intense tone of voice, but couldn't make out specifically what they were saying.

When we were finished in the kitchen and came out to serve coffee, Elizabeth and Hayden smiled in unison. "I have something important to say," Hayden said firmly.

My mother straightened her back and leaned as far forward in the chair as possible.

"We have decided ahead of the usual schedule that Abigail would make an excellent match for our son, Jonah. Because of their young ages, we are proposing a two-year engagement."

I felt my heart beating wildly. Abigail had a blank expression on her face. She wasn't yet even ten years old and most certainly didn't understand to a full extent what the McVeighs were proposing.

It might have been true that she wouldn't actually get married for two more years. Two years sounded like a lifetime to a nine-year-old. She probably thought she would be so much "older" and "mature" by the time she was eleven.

Eleven. It was ridiculous that she was to be married at eleven. Even I knew that.

Had my mother lost her mind? How could she have so eagerly, even happily, agreed to this arrangement? But, of course, saying no or even acting displeased would have brought about terrible repercussions.

# Chapter Twenty-One

The elders were increasingly calling us to more sermons than usual. We were sitting through four, sometimes five, a week now. No matter what the topic of the sermon, the elders always managed to weave into the message that the right thing had been done regarding Whitney Crouse's punishment, and if we didn't watch our own lives as carefully as possible, it could happen to any one of us as well.

Looking back, this was perhaps the most unbelievable aspect of everything that had happened. More incredible than the fact that a teenage girl had been tied to a tree and burned to death was that so many people had been convinced that it was the right thing to do.

Alison tried to explain to us what had happened in Nazi Germany and what propaganda was, and how people could be brainwashed into believing that unthinkable evil was justified. But we didn't know anything about Nazis or propaganda, only that our friend was gone and if we didn't behave appropriately, it could happen to us.

Gathering this frequently in the Community Hall didn't give the dust much chance to accumulate on the pews and between the aisles. But we were required to scrub, wash, and sweep the Community Hall twice a week, no matter how many sermons there were.

With large buckets of vinegar and pine-scented water, we dipped rags into the steamy mixture and began to scrub the floors, the tables, the chairs, and the wooden benches. Each of us had a particular job, and we always kept to the same routine. I started by cleaning the pews on the right side of the room while Alison worked on the left. Lynette always cleaned the area where the elders sat and the pulpit. Katie would start with the floors, and when Lynette was done with the pulpit, she would help her finish.

While our group cleaned the main sanctuary, the other girls in the Preparation who were our age cleaned the front entrance-way, the dining room, and the bathrooms, which were nothing more than indoor outhouses.

Today Katie was late, but we didn't dare wait until she arrived. Cleaning the Community Hall, especially the sermon room, was considered a sacred duty, and if we lagged at all, we would each receive a minor punishment. If one of the elders or their wives saw that we weren't doing our job promptly, we would be forced to skip a meal or run laps around the houses without the benefit of shoes or coats.

When almost ten minutes had passed and she still hadn't shown up, I was starting to get angry. It wasn't fair that she wasn't here to help with this tedious job, and I was surprised that Alison hadn't complained yet. I was about ready to complain for her when Katie came bolting through the front double doors of the Community Hall, nearly out of breath.

She suddenly stopped in the middle of the sanctuary, looking at each of us as if we were the ones who were out of place. Her overalls were stiff and clean-looking, like they had just been washed, dried, and stuffed full of as much starch as they could hold. Her shirt underneath was white as a fluffy cloud and ironed stiff as a board. But her face and hair were a mess.

Without warning, she erupted. "I can't believe they've done this to me! I thought everything would be better, but it's not!"

She paced back and forth while wringing her hands, which were chapped and red. She didn't seem to notice that we all had wet rags in our hands and were busily going about our work.

"It's about time you got here," Alison growled. "Now grab a rag and get to work."

For the first time, I saw a look of pure disgust on Katie's face. But it wasn't directed toward Alison.

"An hour ago, Amy Jo Weber came to my house and announced that she had good news for me."

We all stopped working and looked at Katie. There were only two reasons Amy Jo Weber ever came to anyone's home with good news. Either a baby had just been delivered or an engagement had been made. And we all knew that neither Katie nor anyone in her family had just delivered a baby.

Lynette rushed down from the pulpit and quickly joined the rest of us. "Who is it? Who are you engaged to?"

Katie sucked both lips in at the same time, took a deep breath, and then said the name, "Joey Peterson."

We were all so stunned that even Alison was without words.

"What happened?" I said. "Why did she pair you with Joey?"

Joey Peterson was small, weak, and unattractive. But the more I thought about the match, the more it made sense. Even though Katie was pretty and bright, she was not physically strong or a good athlete.

The elders usually matched individuals with someone similar in size, strength, and athletic prowess. They believed those abilities indicated who would be able to easily reproduce, carry, and bear children without difficulty.

Katie said her parents were nearly crying with joy when it was announced that she was to marry Joey Peterson. Joey was a pimple-faced sixteen-year-old who was so shy I don't think I'd ever heard him talk.

"We'll discuss this more when we're finished," I said, handing Katie a rag. "They'll be checking on us soon, and if we're not working..." I didn't finish because I didn't have to.

She nodded, then took the rag and began cleaning the floor on the east side of the sanctuary, as far away as possible from the rest of us.

I bent down against the bench I'd been polishing, leaning at just the right angle so I could watch Katie's face as she worked. Her eyes were blinking more than normal. But from the nose down, her face didn't move at all, and her lips were closed so tightly I feared if she opened her mouth, she would deflate like a balloon.

And then I thought, perhaps now Katie would want to leave the Community. I knew that as long as Alison was involved with Patrick, she probably wouldn't want to leave. Lynette was terrified of everything and had known nothing outside the Community her entire life. I doubted she would ever want to go, no matter how difficult the circumstances became.

Katie had known enough of what life had been like before, and now, with the prospect of marrying Joey Peterson, perhaps the thoughts of leaving I'd planted in her head were taking root.

I thought about Ross and suddenly felt a stabbing pain in the pit of my stomach. Was it guilt, anxiety, or the fear of actually doing something radical to change my life? Probably all three. I knew I needed to set things right with Ross.

***

The following few days were a whirlwind for Katie. Engagements normally lasted less than six months, and her marriage would be the first in early autumn when the wedding season officially began. Dates had to be set, the menu planned, the wedding party selected, and all the dresses made by hand. The first few days after setting the date were nearly as busy as the last few before the wedding day.

At 8 am sharp on Tuesday morning, Katie was taken to Elizabeth McVeigh's house to be fitted for the wedding gown Elizabeth would sew by hand. There were a lot of not-very-nice things I could say about Elizabeth, but her ability as an expert seamstress was something no one could ever question. And the first dress of the wedding season was always one of the most beautiful. She was excited and seemed to be at her creative best when designing and sewing the first wedding dress.

This was supposed to be a happy time in Katie's life. But it wasn't. A beautiful dress, rows of endless lace, and delicately stitched patterns couldn't erase the emptiness in her heart. The thought of marrying this awkward, scrawny boy she had no feelings for and had barely ever spoken to was unbearable.

As difficult as all this was, it was nothing compared to what was about to happen. I didn't think things could get any worse than what happened with Whitney, but I was wrong.

Less than two days after Katie had announced her engagement to us while we were cleaning the Community Hall, she again came to us with incredible news. During the early morning darkness, the four of us trudged into the woods seeking dry sticks so the Community fires would continue burning.

When we were deep enough into the woods that only the birds and a few small animals could hear us, we stopped and stood in a tight circle. Katie's face was as pale as the bleached sheets that hung every Saturday morning in Elizabeth McVeigh's backyard, and her hair was unkempt and hanging in her face.

Lynette took hold of Katie's tiny hand. "Tell us what happened."

"Last night. It happened last night while I was at the Peterson's. The boys were all out with their dad working in the barns. Mrs. Peterson went to find Joey, so I was alone in the house. That's when Robbie came."

"Robbie came to the Peterson's house?" Lynette said, just above a whisper.

"He knew they were gone. He had to have known."

We each nodded, waiting for her to continue.

"I knew what he wanted as soon as he walked inside and looked at me."

The silence surrounding us when Katie stopped to take a breath was unbearable.

"Robbie's hands were large and calloused. It was like having cold sandpaper against my skin."

She could barely talk about it, but we were all shameless in prying it out of her. Even the cold wind didn't bother us as we waited patiently for each excruciating detail.

Through tears, Katie told us how he pawed like an animal, laughing and smiling while he did it. When he finally got most of her clothes off, the fear of what he was about to do was too much to take, and she finally found the strength to defend herself.

"I just kept scratching and clawing until his big ugly face was bloody. I just couldn't let him have his way with me."

"Good for you," Alison said. "I didn't think you had it in you, Katie Watson."

Lynette was shaking her head the entire time, already knowing such bold behavior would bring nothing but disaster.

"What happened after that?" I asked.

Katie sighed. "He ran away."

"He ran away from you? That's a riot!" Alison said, just as she burst out laughing. It was a nervous, odd sort of laugh.

But Katie wasn't laughing. She wasn't even smiling. In fact, she had started shaking. Lynette put her arms around Katie, rubbing her shoulders.

"What happened after he left?" I asked, almost afraid of what she would say next.

"That's when... when..."

"When what?" Lynette said, gently placing her hand over Katie's.

"When Joey and Mrs. Peterson came in... and saw me naked."

The silence surrounding us dropped like a fallen sycamore.

"But didn't they see Robbie there?" Lynette finally said.

"I guess not. I think he had already gone through the back door. I don't know." She burst out crying.

"It's over now," I said, trying to reassure her.

Katie shook her head, trying to take deep breaths to calm herself. "No, it's not," she stammered. "Because she found me naked, Mrs. Peterson turned me in to the elders. She accused me of trying to seduce her son before the wedding... and of being a witch."

# Chapter Twenty-Two

I packed a basket with several cold chicken sandwiches stuffed with cheddar cheese and a little mustard. Alison had given me a mini bag of potato chips she had gotten from Patrick. I put it in the basket for Ross, along with two large pieces of my mother's chocolate cake.

Hopefully, it would last for more than one day. But I doubted it would since several days had passed since I'd last seen him, and he couldn't have eaten much in that time, if anything at all.

It had only been twenty-four hours since Katie had told us that Joey Peterson and his mother had found her nearly naked in their living room, but it seemed like several days and nights had already come and gone.

The early morning was overwhelmingly quiet and without a trace of wind. There was nothing to fill my ears but the sound of dead twigs and leaves crunching beneath my feet. I carried the basket unhidden at my side.

For the first time since I'd brought anything to Ross, I hadn't come up with an excuse before leaving the house. If someone stopped and questioned me, I would either have to think of something off the top of my head or face the consequences.

It was a good thing I hadn't been stopped or even seen as far as I knew. Even the great fear I'd felt for so long had been worn away with such frustration and anguish that I was certain I would have lashed out at anyone who would have stopped and questioned me, even the great Hayden McVeigh.

When I arrived at the cabin, I was thankful to see a tiny, nearly imperceptible fire burning outside. If someone saw the smoke, those in the Community would never even think that a Black man on the run for his life was staying there. Anything out of the ordinary that happened now was attributed to the nonexistent witches. I was cold and looking forward to warming myself at the fire.

I suddenly remembered that the last time I'd spoken to Ross, I'd told him we weren't interested in his help, didn't want to leave the Community, and that he should go as soon as he was well. I didn't mean those things anymore, but my pride didn't want to come out and immediately tell him so.

I saw him before he saw me. He was sitting on a log in front of the fire, staring into the flames. I tried to imagine what the last several weeks had been like for him, hiding in the greenhouse and then moving to the cabin, injured, alone, and hungry.

He'd gone from one desperate situation to another, dependent upon me to bring him food and medicine. I felt terrible for being so harsh with him, especially now that I knew we had to leave the Community. Soon, I would very likely become dependent upon him.

When he finally saw me, he instantly smiled and stood up. I'm sure his happiness at seeing me had little to do with the expectation of enjoying my company, especially since I'd been so unkind the last time we'd spoken, and more to do with the fact that I was carrying a basket.

"Is it okay if I come and sit with you?" I said.

"Of course." He pointed to a dry spot on the log.

"I've brought you some food." I pushed the basket toward him, giving him permission to begin eating. I was certain he devoured the first sandwich and the bag of chips in less than a minute. He didn't say a word until he began to unwrap the first piece of cake, and only because he needed something to fill the space between us while he awkwardly pulled off the paper wrapping.

"This is really good. Thank you so much."

That was it. I couldn't take it anymore.

"I'm sorry I was mean to you the last time I was here. I was just confused and upset when I found out about the robbery. I'm sorry. I don't want you to leave. At least not yet."

It took him two swallows to get all the cake he'd stuffed in his mouth down. When he could talk again, he assured me that he wasn't angry. "I didn't blame you for being upset. You don't owe me anything, and look how much you've already done for me."

He was so calm about it all. Most people would be angry and unforgiving if they hadn't eaten for more than a day.

"Your leg is almost healed. Are you planning on leaving soon? If you are, I have something to talk to you about," I said.

I had assumed, up until the last time I'd seen him, that he'd want to leave. Knowing he was a fugitive, I saw the impossible position that he was in. He could either turn himself in and possibly spend years in prison or live as a fugitive in the woods near the Community. And if the elders ever found out he was here, prison might very well look like a good alternative.

"I am going to leave. I'm waiting another week, though."

"Why?"

"There'll be a full moon in a week. It will be easier to make my way to Wheatland."

I nodded slowly, thinking how long a week could be in the Community. Katie was in trouble, and there was no telling what could transpire in even a few days.

He must have noticed my troubled expression. "I want you to help me escape when you leave. I know it's a lot to ask and could put you in danger."

"Of course, I'll help you," he said.

He picked up the basket with the rest of the food. "Come inside. We'll sit at the table and talk."

While he ate, he intermittently explained what he thought was the best way to reach Wheatland on foot. When I suggested taking either the truck or the van from the Community, he looked surprised.

"Do you know where the keys are?"

"No. I assume they're always with either Jonathon or Hayden. I'm sure they wouldn't be easy to find."

Ross smiled. "It's not something to be proud of, but I know how to hot-wire a car."

I was suddenly excited and hopeful that we might be able to pull this off. Knowing this about Ross made me curious to find out more about him.

"Tell me something about yourself, just anything," I said.

He tilted his head and looked out the dirty cabin window. It was like he thought traces of himself were left out there near the smoldering flames. When he realized there wasn't, he looked at me and reached into his back pocket. "I don't know if there's anything else to tell you, but I can show you."

He handed me a picture of himself with his arm around an older woman. I could tell by looking at her that she was his mother.

"That's my momma," he said, handing me the picture.

I smiled. There were a thousand stories in this one picture, and I wanted to hear them all. I suddenly knew so many more things about him just by looking at this one moment in time.

The way his mother stood, holding her chin up and her shoulders back, I knew she was a strong woman who had worked hard her whole life and had raised him right. The way he had his hand around her shoulder, I knew how much he loved her and that she would always think of him as her baby.

"That's a nice picture," I said, handing it back.

"Tell me, how are things with you? How are things in the Community?" He took a large bite of the second sandwich and then stretched out his legs as if he were waiting for a lengthy story. He was right about that, and if I told him how everything really was with me or the Community, he would have to eat more than one sandwich for me to finish the story.

"Things aren't good, not really. But you already knew that. How is your leg?" I tried to keep my answer short and simple and move on to something else. But when he leaned forward again and looked at me with such sadness in his eyes, everything came spilling out at once.

"My friend, Katie, is in serious trouble. I'm afraid of what might happen to her."

He squeezed my hand and nodded. Unfortunately, he knew what I meant and that there wasn't any need to discuss it further.

"I guess in different ways, we're both broken people," he said, looking at me as if he could see straight into my soul at all the damage that had been done. "Your misery was brought about by others; mine I brought on myself."

"But you didn't kill that man," I said with conviction because I knew in my heart that he didn't.

He tried to contain how happy he was that I'd said that, but he couldn't. His eyes became cloudy and full of tears, but he didn't cry. "No, I didn't kill that man, but I robbed his store. And if I hadn't been there along with Robert, that man might still be alive."

"But you don't know that."

"That's exactly right. I don't know that. But the uncertainty is what I'll have to live with the rest of my life."

I thought about how he'd said the name of the other man, probably without even realizing it.

"So, if you didn't shoot that man... did Robert?"

He suddenly looked terribly upset. He swallowed and sniffed a couple of times, doing everything he could to keep from crying. It took him several seconds to finally build up enough strength to speak again. "Yes, Robert shot him." He couldn't look at me when he said it, and I could only imagine that he and Robert had been very close.

"Who is Robert?" I asked.

"Robert is my brother."

***

"Sit still! I can't get the stitching straight if you keep moving around so much."

Lynette stitched together the skin on Alison's leg while I steadied her by leaning onto her shoulders. Alison was strong, and Lynette was getting better at the art of being a nurse, but Alison would still be left with a large scar on her lower left leg.

She had attempted to lift an extraordinary amount of weight during the lifting competitions. When the metal bar she'd been holding slipped from her hands, it fell along the back of her calf, leaving a large gash before crashing into the ground.

"As bad as this is, at least you didn't break an arm," I said somberly, referring to what had happened to Adalei Wilson.

"It really needs a few more stitches, which means I need to get some more thread," Lynette said.

"We don't have time," Alison insisted. "We have to get dressed and be at the Community Hall in less than twenty minutes."

The elders had called an impromptu gathering that evening. This rarely happened, but when it did, it was often to announce good news. Tonight, we could look forward to music, dancing, and lots of food. We dressed and prepared quickly that evening.

Katie had not been at the competitions earlier, and she was not at the Community Hall when we arrived. Yet I hadn't heard a word about what had happened to her. I wouldn't have even known that anything was wrong, only that she was missing, if she hadn't told us what had happened while we were gathering sticks.

The drums, a banjo, and a few acoustic guitars didn't look like much arranged haphazardly in the corner of the Community Hall. But when the Davis brothers began to play them, it turned into a musical jamboree with dancing and singing and loud clapping.

As soon as the music began, with a combination of country, bluegrass, and old-time Gospel, Terrance O'Malley pulled me onto the dance floor. He pressed his thin body next to mine, and we began to spin around as if we were one person.

"Am I holding your hand too tightly?" he said awkwardly.

My face was pressed into his chest. "No."

Of course, he was holding on way too tightly. Even though I wasn't interested in him in the least bit, I didn't want him to let go. For some reason, I felt safe and secure while this scrawny boy held onto me. It wasn't long before the entire room was filled with dancing couples. I closed my eyes and burrowed into Terrance's chest. His beating heart pounded against my cheek.

I was able to temporarily numb my mind with dancing and music, believing things might stay relatively sane enough for us to hold on until we could escape. Then Hayden McVeigh suddenly signaled for the music to stop. He made his way to the podium and cleared his throat.

"We are getting ready to begin the joyous season of engagements. In the fall, we will embark upon an even happier time of attending weddings and watching our young people in the Preparation begin their new lives as married couples."

I looked around the room. I could see smiles everywhere. But Elizabeth McVeigh, in particular, had a wider smile on her face than I could ever remember.

"It is a bit unusual for a young lady to become engaged before entering the Preparation. But this year, an exceptional young girl has been chosen to not only become engaged but to marry into the McVeigh family."

I felt my stomach twist into a thousand knots. Everyone was smiling, clapping, and looking around in anticipation of the chosen girl.

"Abigail Sawyer has been chosen to be the bride of my son, Jonah!" he exclaimed.

That night, I wept as I sat on my bed in near darkness and opened the Bible. I had recently been reading from the Book of Romans. This particular night, I was in Romans 10 when I read out loud verse 13.

*For whosoever shall call upon the name of the Lord shall be saved.*

I said the words out loud, "This place is a mess. I'm a mess. Jesus, save me."

I suddenly felt overwhelming peace and contentment. I knew, whatever happened from this moment, that I'd be okay.

## Counselor

This is the first time since I've been in counseling that my predominant emotion is no longer fear.

"That you're finally getting angry about what happened at the Community shows that you're making progress," the counselor says firmly. "Before this, I don't think you've expressed anything but fear. You're beginning to come to terms with what happened and grasping how outrageous it was."

The woman in the front room is no longer typing. I can't hear any file cabinets opening or closing. There are no footsteps or small bits of conversation. There's nothing external to hold onto or filter out what I've just remembered. I begin to breathe heavily again, feeling trapped by the memory.

I stretch my back and lean forward. "I know now that the night after visiting Ross was a turning point," I say somberly. "Both in my time at the Community and spiritually."

# Chapter Twenty-Three

It took less than twenty-four hours for Katie's engagement to be canceled and for the elders to banish her to the Community Hall basement. She was forced to live there until her trial for indecent exposure and witchcraft.

The trial would have occurred immediately, as had Whitney's, if not for the fact that pipes in one of the water wells had burst and an emergency well had to be dug. It would take at least a dozen Community men and a couple of days to dig and construct a new well. Katie would be held in seclusion until then.

As strict as life had been in the Community before the incident with Katie, it became even more unbearable after. A somberness fell over our lives as thick as the gray clouds hovering overhead. Each breath I took was labored and slow. I barely slept and was hardly able to eat. I was floating like smoke from the Community Hall to the greenhouse and then back home again.

The only time I was able to crawl out of the suffocating bubble that had trapped all of us inside was when I was in my bed reading the Bible or locked up tight in the greenhouse. Everything else didn't seem real.

Early the next morning, I snuck out of the house and brought Ross some soup, bread, and cheese. I was thankful to find him sleeping. As much as I needed his companionship and conversation, I wasn't ready to face what would come next between us. He'd already told me that he was leaving soon. I had to make a final decision within a few days. I left the food on the table in the cabin and returned home to the warmth of my bed.

A few days later, after the new well was finished and water was pumping again for cooking, cleaning, and bathing, we all waited for the elders to bring Katie out for the trial. It was to begin at exactly two o'clock in the Community Hall. Even though it was still cold outside, the heat inside was stifling.

The doors behind where we were all sitting opened and then closed. One set of footsteps was deep and hard, the other soft and light, and sounded as if they were broken and uneven.

When Katie was finally brought before the congregation, I gasped. She looked awful. She had dark circles under her eyes and a deep chest cough that made her whole body shake. I knew she hadn't bathed or washed her hair in at least four days.

Jonathon Alden helped her into the chair next to the podium, while Hayden McVeigh cleared his throat and prepared to speak. He didn't waste any time getting right to the point.

"The young woman sitting before you has been charged with indecent exposure, seduction... and witchcraft. She was found fully unclothed in the Peterson home by Mrs. Peterson and her son, Joseph!"

He paused for a few seconds to give everyone time to gasp and murmur among themselves. Hayden McVeigh knew how to present his case with dramatic flair.

"Is there anyone here who can stand in defense of Katherine Marie Watson?" Hayden McVeigh declared.

It was the only time I'd heard Katie's full name pronounced. Her full name being laid bare before the entire Community inspired me to rise to my feet. But silence and fear, as heavy as a lead weight, kept my mouth from opening. Elder McVeigh was facing the other side of the Hall and hadn't seen me stand or my mother grab hold of my arm and try to pull me back down.

"There are no witnesses! There is no defense for a liar, a witch, and a seductress!" Hayden McVeigh yelled across the room.

"That's not true," I finally said.

Again, murmuring filled the room as my mother let go, and Hayden McVeigh spun around with a brutal glare in his eyes. When he turned and looked straight at me, I was certain there was enough power in those eyes to cause me to collapse and melt into the wooden bench beneath me. I whispered the name "Jesus" just loud enough that only my mother could hear, and somehow I not only remained standing but had the strength to open my mouth and speak.

"I can testify that Katie was only defending herself against Robbie McVeigh and that she wasn't seducing Joey Peterson."

Jonathon Alden stood up, and the entire room became so quiet that I could hear myself breathe. "You will be our first witness tomorrow at 8 am, Miss Sawyer."

***

I woke before Abigail the following morning and carefully crawled out of bed so I wouldn't disturb her. After quickly dressing, I planned to grab a piece of bread and some cheese and be out the door before anyone else was up. I was going to the Community Hall before the others arrived. I would sit in the pews by myself, praying and begging God for strength while waiting for Katie's trial to begin.

I'd just taken a piece of bread and stuffed the first bite in my mouth when I heard what sounded like falling and crashing sounds coming from the bathroom. As I stuffed the remainder of the bread and a piece of cheese into my pocket and hurried to the bathroom, my mother called for me to help her back to bed.

"What happened? Did you fall?"

My mother held onto the sink with one hand and clutched her stomach with the other. "I'm sick. I'm not sure if it's the flu or something I ate, but my stomach hurts something awful."

I couldn't imagine that something she ate had made her sick. The three of us had eaten at home the night before and had all eaten the same thing. I put my arm around her waist and guided her back to the bedroom. "It's probably the stomach flu. I'll tell Abigail to make you some tea before I leave."

There was a look of horror on her face. "No, tea won't be strong enough. You need to see Jada right away. She'll know what to make for me."

Jada brewed a home remedy consisting of lemon, ginger, and several other secret ingredients we could never quite figure out. But I didn't have time to wait for her to make the remedy. It would take at least an hour, and that was if she had all the ingredients.

"You have to send Abigail," I insisted. "I have to testify for Katie, and the trial is going to start soon."

She grabbed my arm and squeezed. "Abigail was up last night sick, too. Don't wake her. We both need this remedy. You can go to the trial after you bring it back for us."

I looked at her face, so full of pain, and then thought of Abigail being sick as well.

"Okay," I finally said. I ran as quickly as I could to Jada's home. Both Lynette and her grandmother were up when I arrived. I explained my mother's situation and then pleaded with Jada to make the concoction as quickly as possible so I could testify at the trial.

"Don't worry, dear," Jada said, with more comfort and compassion than I could ever remember. "I'll get it done as quickly as possible."

She told Lynette to go to the trial and inform the elders that my mother was sick, that she was fixing a remedy, and that I would be there to testify as soon as I had delivered the medicine to my mother.

While Jada was in the kitchen getting the ingredients ready, I went to Lynette's room. She had just pulled a blue sweatshirt over her overalls when I grabbed her by the shoulders. "If I don't get there in time, you'll have to speak up for Katie."

She shook her head adamantly. "I never said I would do that. I'm not sure why you did." She backed away from me. "I'll tell them you'll be there as soon as possible."

By the time Jada finished making the remedy and poured it into a mason jar, almost an hour had passed. I hurried home, running between the houses and through backyards as quickly as I could.

I came into the front room to find Abigail on the sofa knitting.

"Abigail, should you even be out of bed?"

She put down her knitting and made a strange face. "Why shouldn't I be out of bed?"

I sat next to her, admiring the effortless beauty of the quilt she was working on. "Weren't you up sick last night?"

"No. Why would you think that?"

It took only a few seconds to understand what had happened. My head was spinning, maybe even worse than when I'd smelled Whitney's flesh disintegrating into the north meadow. I could hardly believe my mother was capable of such deceit.

"Never mind," I said, leaning forward and looking into the kitchen. I saw the back door slightly open. My mother must have been outside, retrieving something from the icebox.

"Make sure Mom gets this," I said, setting Jada's remedy on the sofa next to Abigail. "I've got to get to the Community Hall."

Within seconds of shutting the front door, I heard my mother's footsteps pounding across the living room floor inside the house. She threw open the front door and called after me. "Hannah! Come back!"

I started running and didn't look back until I was inside the Community Hall. Despite what she'd done, I couldn't blame my mother. She'd lost her husband, and now mothers were losing their daughters in the Community.

I pushed my way through the double doors of the Community Hall and ran toward the sanctuary. Before I could stop, I ran straight into Hayden McVeigh. It felt as if I'd crashed into a brick wall. He hunted bear, bison, and antelope nearly every morning before dawn and spent several hours after that swinging an ax or a hammer. Though well into his fifties, the man was pure muscle.

He laid his large hands on my shoulders and slowly pushed me back. "And where are you heading in such a hurry?"

I swallowed and then forced the words out. "I came to testify for Katie." My voice squeaked when I spoke.

"The trial is over," he said briskly. "Your mother is sick. Now get home where you belong, girl."

The trial was over before I arrived. It had been much shorter than Whitney's, and everyone knew the outcome before it was over. I hesitated for only a moment before turning around and running all the way back home.

# Chapter Twenty-Four

That night, I tried to keep myself warm by pulling the blankets off Abigail as much as possible without waking her. When I finally realized that attempting to sleep was useless, I quietly got out of bed, dressed, and did the unthinkable. I snuck out of the house in the middle of the night.

Even though I hadn't consciously planned ahead of time where I'd be going, something had propelled me forward. Something I didn't entirely understand pulled me like a magnet through the cool spring wind and the blackness of a night virtually hidden by a new moon. I ended up along the main road, staring at the Community Hall.

I'd never known until this moment whether the doors were locked on the Community buildings on the main road during the night or not. I guess I had assumed they wouldn't be since those in our homes didn't have locks, even if we had wanted to use them. But the door was locked.

I started walking around the building, searching for a way to get inside, finally realizing for the first time why I was here. My mind must have been thinking about it for hours, but now was the first time it came into conscious thought. I had to see Katie. I had to talk to her about my faith in Jesus Christ.

One of the ground-level windows that led into the basement had been left slightly open. It could have been left ajar for weeks or even months without anyone noticing. In all likelihood, it had been opened sometime during warmer weather and simply hadn't been closed again. Bending down into a patch of brittle weeds and slush, I managed to pry it completely open.

I slipped through the narrow opening between the frozen ground and the top of the window, dropping into the basement. If I had weighed much more than 110 pounds, I don't think I would have made it through. But overeating or not working to the point of exhaustion were not options in the Community, and so I was rail thin.

For a second or two, I sat on the cement floor, waiting to be found out, caught, and held in seclusion as well. When I realized nothing was around me but silence and darkness, I knew I had successfully made my way inside.

I had no idea where Katie was, and there was very little light to guide me. Pale, yellowish strands of light from the moon filtered through the top of the window. This dungeon of a basement, the underground of the Community Hall, was in stark contrast to the pristine, white-washed areas above that we kept scrubbed and cleaned regularly.

It couldn't have been more than fifty or fifty-five degrees. The concrete walls held in the cold like large chunks of ice. There were several rooms in the basement to search. The first room

I was in contained a few boxes and trunks lined up against the walls.

"Katie?" I called, barely above a whisper, while I was in the hall between rooms. I stopped and waited for a reply, and then started walking again when I didn't get one.

The second and third rooms I explored held furniture, tools, and equipment used to run the Community. The fourth room I entered contained only a mattress on the floor and what looked like a pile of blankets scattered haphazardly on top.

I would have left this room as well if it hadn't been for the slight movement under the blankets. This curled-up ball moving underneath had to be Katie.

"Katie?" I touched the bottom part of the blanket that had moved and pushed gently. Whatever was underneath squirmed again, then stopped. "Katie?"

She suddenly bolted up, looked straight at me, and screamed.

"Don't yell! Someone will hear us!"

She flew off the mattress and threw her arms around me. "Is it you? Are you really here?"

I pulled her forward so the light through the small window illuminated our faces. The yellowish light caused her to look ghostly, with strange and uneven features.

"I just had to come see you and talk to you," I said quickly.

I could see Katie's eyes narrow in the strange light. "Talk to me about what?"

"I want to make sure if... if..."

"If what?" Katie said.

"If you die, you'll go to heaven."

She didn't even argue with me or dispute the fact that she would soon die. Eternity was the only topic that was left to talk about.

"But I've been baptized and I'm a member of the Community Church."

"I know, and it's good that you've been baptized, but there's more they haven't told us."

She looked confused, as if she didn't understand what I was saying, or didn't want to.

"I don't think that the elders here are really being led by God," I said softly.

Katie's face turned ash gray. "You can't say something like that," she whispered.

I recited Romans 10:9-10

*That if thou shalt confess with thy mouth the Lord Jesus, and shalt believe in thine heart that God hath raised him from the dead, thou shalt be saved. For with the heart man believeth unto righteousness; and with the mouth confession is made unto salvation.*

"If we're good and follow the teachings of the Community, we'll go to heaven," Katie said somberly. Her words were faint and uneven, and I knew she wasn't sure if what she said was right.

"No, that's not true." I squeezed her hand and said the words again, hoping they would sink into her soul.

"The Community believes in Jesus," she insisted.

"I don't think it's in the same way this verse is talking about."

She pulled away from me. "So, you're saying we don't have to be good? We don't have to obey anything?"

"Of course, we should try to be good and obey, but that's not what ultimately saves us. Truly accepting Christ and what he did on the cross is what saves us."

Something took root in Katie at that moment, and I knew she was beginning to understand.

She leaned towards me. "Say the verse again."

She closed her eyes while I again spoke the words of life.

***

The sun was rising when I quietly made my way back into the house.

"I have to talk to you," I told Abigail as soon as I was home.

She wiped the sleep from her eyes and slowly sat up. I wasn't sure where to even begin, so I started by making her promise not to tell a soul what I was about to say to her.

After that, I opened my mouth and let it fall out, one sentence, one fact at a time. Ross... a fugitive... hiding in the cabin and wanted for murder... but he didn't do it... he's going to help us leave the Community.

For several seconds, she looked at me with an expression of complete shock coupled with confusion. This I had expected. But then her entire face lit up, and she broke into a smile. That, I had not anticipated.

She nodded slowly, still smiling. "Good, I want to leave," she said just above a whisper. "Please take me with you."

I realized later how unusual it was for a child her age to want to leave without even asking about our mother. But so deep was her desire to flee the Community that the first mention of the possibility of it caused her to immediately want to go.

"Okay, I don't know for sure when it will happen," I said. "And you absolutely cannot tell another soul that Ross is staying at the cabins. Not even our mother. I'll tell her myself when the time is right."

"I promise. I promise," she said quickly.

***

That evening, the news was delivered throughout the Community by the elderly women. Katie had officially been declared guilty, and judgment was passed.

That night, as my tears soaked the pillow, I begged God to do something. In frustration, I dared Him to show himself. I dared Him to come to the Community and fight the evil that had set itself up against Him.

I had slept an hour, maybe two at the most. It was a fitful sleep that I was awakened from by the sound of running water and a clanging coffee kettle in the kitchen. My mother must not have slept well either. She did little more than stare out the window and drink coffee for most of the morning.

When it was time to leave, I didn't argue or hesitate. We had done this before. I knew the routine. This, in some strange way, made it easier to bear, at least in the beginning.

I walked beside my mother and those around me without much thought, and without even looking toward the north meadow where we were going. I studied the few patches of snow that remained on the dry, brittle ground while concentrating on each cold breath, one after the other.

For a short while, I actually believed I could get through this without any conscious thought. I could focus on the ground, the sky, and the air in my lungs, and come back without any real memory of what happened. But that would ultimately prove to be ridiculous.

I concentrated as hard as I could not to see, not to hear, but I wasn't strong enough. The smell was overwhelming, sickeningly acidic, like rotten meat on an overheated grill. I tried to breathe through my shirt, even my hair, but nothing could filter the horrifying aroma of Katie's incinerated flesh.

Then I remembered – that's when I tried to run away, at least get to the back of the crowd, back where breathing, living bodies could serve as a barrier between me and that horrendous odor. But they wouldn't let me go. As soon as I turned, trying to make my way to the back, Hayden McVeigh grabbed me by the collar of my shirt.

"Oh no, my dear. You've earned yourself a ticket to the front row, and that's where you'll stay until there's nothing left but ashes."

"No!" I screamed as he pulled me as close as possible to the flames.

I knew screaming was useless, as no one would help me, not even my mother. Whenever Hayden or Jonathon gave an order, they all became mannequins, as stiff and useless as wooden dolls.

And so I remained in the front, Hayden McVeigh's thick hands around the back of my neck. The wind shifted, and the smoke covered my eyes. And I thanked God that even though my eyes felt as if they were on fire, I could no longer see.

As the tears ran down my face, those who saw me must have thought I was crying for Katie. But Katie's pain was over now. I was crying for the rest of us.

## Counselor

It took more effort for my mind to retrieve the image of Katie's burned body than of Whitney's. The picture ran through my brain like a jittery movie reel, disappearing and then replaying again. Like intense labor pains, coming and going in my mind, when the picture hits with full force, I scream and try desperately to rid myself of the image.

"Let yourself remember," the counselor says. "You have to fight through this. It's the only way to get past the most intense pain."

The counselor pages the nurse, telling her to bring in a sedative. I don't want to take it. I'm afraid I'll fall asleep and have nightmares for hours. I'm afraid of hearing Katie scream again as she burns to death.

"You're not going to fall asleep. I promise," she says. "It will just help you relax."

I reluctantly swallow the pill with a small amount of water. Within a few minutes, the edges begin to drop off the saw blades in my brain. The images are still there, but they are cloudy, and I can bear them.

"Can you see Katie?" the counselor asks.

I nod. But the picture in my mind grows cloudier, and what I think is the smoke from the Burning Tree, I soon realize, are the tears in my eyes. I open my eyes, and she's gone.

The only consolation I have is that I believe she had truly accepted and committed her life to following Christ the night before her death. Katie's misery is over, but so much of mine is just beginning.

The counselor puts her arms around me and squeezes as she sighs. It's the first time she's shown any emotion since I've been coming here. When my aunt comes to pick me up, I'm calm and breathing easily.

The counselor whispers something to my aunt. They talk for a few more seconds before the counselor returns. They decide it's best if Aunt Vicky waits outside while we finish.

# Chapter Twenty-Five

I wondered how the others in the Community emotionally survived what had happened. How did they make it from one sunrise to the next without going crazy? Then I realized they weren't. In the presence of each other, and especially the elders, everyone tightly secured their masks and played their roles as best they could.

After Whitney had been put to death, there was anxiety, sleeplessness, and excessive drinking. What was happening now was even worse. Couples were fighting, and there were rumors of physical abuse, but it was mostly kept behind closed doors. Even so, along with the chaos, there was a silence that covered the Community, darker than fear.

I continued to secretly read the Bible, burying verses in my heart like hidden treasure. Later, I would retrieve them and cling to each word like the last drops of water in an endless desert. I looked around and saw how the others who didn't have such a foundation were faring. They were fading fast.

Faint whispers were heard in the general store and along the main road after Community services and events. People were considering leaving the Community and returning to Denver, Cheyenne, Kansas City, and every other place they had come from. Of course, no one ever came out and said they were leaving. People talked about hearing of other families who heard about someone else who was thinking of leaving.

When the elders heard the rumors, the entire Community had been called for an impromptu sermon. When Hayden McVeigh stepped onto the platform, I don't think I'd ever seen him look like he did that evening. He wore a silk black suit, a coal-black tie, and shiny black shoes, each as black as the sky under a new moon. His face was pale, cleanly shaven, and smelling of Elizabeth's homemade soap.

"The tree... that refuses to burn!" He hesitated before continuing, making sure he had everyone's full attention.

The Burning Tree. That glorious, frightful tree that refused to burn always seemed to capture the attention of every single member of the Community. Its ability to survive amazing circumstances, as well as the supernatural aura that surrounded the tree, kept it an endless object of fascination.

"Because the tree is a sign from God... we all must stay here and work through the sin and sadness that has engulfed our precious Community."

His voice had changed, sounding so different from what I had ever remembered.

"But if we leave now and try to flee from our responsibilities and the Community we have worked so hard to build together, the wrath of the tree will surely follow."

He was telling us that to leave now would mean we should expect trouble, even disaster, and most assuredly, the wrath of the Burning Tree. Then his expression, voice, and even the color of his cheeks changed again. He smiled slightly, which I had never before seen from the podium. "There is a way out," he said, barely above a whisper.

Hayden McVeigh leaned onto the podium with all of his weight. It looked like he was trying to bury the podium into the ground beneath him. He explained that all matches would be made and engagements set by the end of the week. He finally stopped smiling as he said it, but his voice never changed.

There was never a sound during one of the elder's sermons. But the moment he said that all engagements would be set by the end of the week, murmuring flowed throughout the Community Hall.

Hayden McVeigh leaned back again, not appearing the least bit angry but merely pleased that he had managed to shock the congregation into breaking one of his own rules.

"This is a good thing," my mother said when we returned home after the service. That Elder McVeigh had ended his fire and brimstone sermon on what she perceived as a positive note seemed to make her happy. I tried to pretend that I didn't hear her. But she kept talking, becoming more excited as the words spilled out of her mouth.

That evening, my mother talked incessantly about planning my wedding and how she was so excited that everything was happening ahead of schedule. She even started talking to Abigail about being in my wedding, telling her that if the elders didn't consider her still young enough to be a flower girl, she could be a bridesmaid.

She stared into the steam as it rose from the beef she was cooking and buried her face in the warm fog. Did she think she could lose herself in the fog and keep pretending? I didn't know much about denial, but enough to know my mother was in it. I let her keep pretending, occasionally nodding and smiling as if I were paying attention. Telling her there wouldn't be a wedding would only cause trouble I couldn't deal with.

A few hours later, as the sun set over the Community, Lynette, Alison, and I gathered twigs and brush at the edge of the woods. We loaded the wheelbarrow with what we had gathered and realized we'd need to spend more time to collect the same amount as usual.

"We have to get more," Lynette complained.

"That's right," Alison said. "There are only three of us now. It will take longer to get the same amount of work done."

I stopped walking and said in a voice louder than I had anticipated, "Don't you realize what's happening? They're getting rid of us one by one."

Alison laughed, but it wasn't funny laughter. "No kidding, Einstein. And what exactly are we supposed to do about it?"

There was something different about Alison today. There was a sadness about her that I hadn't noticed before.

"You know what we can do about it. We can leave, all of us together!" I said.

"Stop!" Lynette screamed. "Stop talking like that! Do you want us all to die?"

Alison dropped the twigs in her arms before leaning against a small cottonwood tree, wrapping her arms around it to steady herself.

"What's wrong?" I asked.

"I think I'm going to be sick."

I pulled strands of hair away from her face as she leaned over and threw up. She took slow, deep breaths and then bent over and threw up again in the leaves.

"We need to take you to Ruth Anne," Lynette said.

Alison scrambled to stand without the aid of the tree before Lynette or I could suggest it a second time. "No. Are you crazy? We don't need to draw any more attention to ourselves. Besides, I'm okay."

"Why are you sick?" I said the words slowly and evenly, trying not to rile up Alison or worry Lynette.

Alison shook her head. "I don't know. I guess it had to be the dinner. None of those girls working in the kitchen for the Preparation know how to cook."

"That's the truth," Lynette said, adding an exaggerated sigh.

Perhaps that was it, nothing more than a bad meal and, of course, the stress of being a young, single girl in the Community.

Then, without warning, Alison stepped next to me, so close I could smell the vomit still on her breath. "Is Ross still planning on leaving soon? Is he still at the cabins?"

Lynette and I looked at one another for a second. "Yes, as far as I know," I said.

As soon as I had spoken, I felt light raindrops on my face. The sprinkles quickly increased to heavy rain.

The heavy downpour would keep everyone in the Community inside for several hours, making it the perfect time for the three of us to go to the cabins. Even so, it was dangerous for all of us to be gone at one time. Despite the pouring rain, we would gather as many sticks for kindling on our way there and the way back as possible.

I was practically running as I pushed the wheelbarrow down the narrow path. I stopped occasionally to let Lynette and Alison make sure the tarp was securely covering the sticks inside the wheelbarrow. Pellets of rain beat against my face while mud soaked my shoes and socks past my ankles. By the time we made it to the cabin, the wheelbarrow was still half empty.

When Ross saw all three of us standing at the door, he quickly ushered us inside. His leg was completely healed, and he was now able to walk briskly. There were, however, shadows under his eyes, and I thought perhaps he hadn't slept well recently.

"These are my friends, Lynette and Alison," I said, pointing to each one.

Lynette had never seen a Black man in her entire life. And although I told her not to stare, she seemed incapable of stopping.

"I'm glad to finally meet you," he said. "Let's sit down and talk."

We immediately gathered around the small table, and Ross asked in a stern, low voice if we were ready to leave the Community.

"Yes," I said eagerly.

Lynette suddenly became very nervous. "I'm not sure. I just came to hear what you had to say."

"Fair enough, but we don't have much time. If you decide to come with me, I want you to know I'll be leaving in less than a week."

"The elders are planning on having us all married within a few weeks," Alison said with a hint of sarcasm.

Ross looked surprised, and then asked, "Are the marriages in the Community even legal?"

"Hayden McVeigh and Jonathon Alden are both licensed ministers in the state of Wyoming," Lynette said.

Ross shook his head. "But for a marriage to be legal, the couples have to fill out a marriage license, get blood tests, and things like that."

"Last year, which was the first year I was here for the wedding season, they did all that," Alison said. "I remember they loaded up the couples in the Community van and took them to Cheyenne to get everything like that done."

"I doubt they'll do that this year," I said softly. "I don't think they'll let anyone leave after what's happened."

Ross shook his head again. "I don't know. They might if they keep everyone supervised. But even if they don't, they'll almost certainly carry out the weddings with or without the consent of the state. But I've got a plan to get us all out," Ross exclaimed, sounding almost cheerful as he said it. "I decided how we would leave... if we all went together."

"What's your plan?" Alison said. She had been watching Ross intently since we came to the cabin, watching his expressions and listening to his every word. She must have finally decided that she could trust him.

"The Community has a van, right?" Ross asked.

"And a pickup truck," Alison added.

"What kind of vehicles are they?" he asked. "Ford? Chevrolet? Toyota?"

"The truck's a Ford and the van is a Chevy," I said.

A faint smile crept across his face. "It looks like we're taking the truck. I don't know how to hot-wire a Chevy."

"We're stealing the elder's truck?" Lynette said.

Ross looked at Lynette like she was crazy for feeling guilty about taking the truck. Not that stealing wasn't wrong, of course it was. But in light of what was happening in the Community and the danger we all faced, I hoped God would overlook it in this instance.

"We're borrowing it," Ross said with a smile. "They can have it back when we're done using it."

"The truck has a back seat, so the five of us should be able to fit," I said.

"The five of us?" Ross said.

"I've decided I'm taking my little sister, Abigail, with us when we leave."

# Chapter Twenty-Six

I t was now early April, and the landscape was beginning to change. The Laramie Mountains were a splattering of paint box watercolors in pastel pink, baby blue, and eggshell yellow. Only the tops were covered with pristine white snow.

The mountains looked so beautiful and peaceful, and I imagined myself living there, snug and safe under a blanket of pearly snow. I wondered what it would be like to meet God at the top of the mountain, like Moses had met Him on Mount Sinai.

"What are you thinking about?" Lynette asked as the three of us left the outer limits of the Community.

"How beautiful the mountains are in spring. And how I imagine God is up among the peaks."

Lynette smiled briefly, but the smile quickly faded. She had not come to know God in the same way I had.

The wheelbarrow I was pushing was only about half full of sticks when the rain started. The warmer weather had brought rain almost daily during the last week. It was light at first, and we kept gathering wood at a steady pace. After a few minutes, it increased so that all three of us were becoming noticeably wet.

"I think we should go back," Lynette said.

"But we need to talk about Ross," I said.

Lynette frowned. "If the wood gets too wet, we'll have to throw it out and start all over again. And we don't have a tarp with us."

I took my jacket off and placed it over the wood, making it clear I wanted to stay here and discuss what we needed to do, no matter how much it rained. Lynette was flustered that I'd so easily come up with a way to keep the wood dry.

I looked at Alison. She was now standing several yards away from us. She tilted her head back, letting the light rain wash against her face. Alison had acted so strangely during the last several days. Acting strange was perhaps not the right word. Maybe wishy-washy and indecisive were better ways to describe her behavior.

She initially acted as if she were as repelled by Patrick and Robbie as the rest of us. Then, she denied any involvement with Patrick when I confronted her. After that, when she finally admitted it, she acted as if she wanted to carry on a secret affair with him indefinitely. Then, unexpectedly, she had been as eager as anyone else to escape the Community. Today, she was distant and didn't seem interested in anything we talked about.

Suddenly, the rain increased to a soft but steady pour. It wouldn't be long before my jacket would no longer be enough to keep the wood dry.

"We have to go back," Lynette insisted.

"Take the wheelbarrow to the shed. We'll meet up with you in a little bit," I instructed.

Without complaint, Lynette began pushing the wheelbarrow back toward the Community, leaving Alison and me standing in the clearing.

"Come with me," I said, grabbing Alison's hand. Without a word, she followed behind me like a small child. For her to mindlessly follow along without even questioning where we were going only caused me to walk even faster. I had to know what had happened to change her usual vibrant and rebellious demeanor.

When I found the spot I was looking for, I sat on the closest log, pulling Alison down next to me. We were under an umbrella of new spring leaves that kept out most of the rain.

"You have to tell me what's going on." My hand held onto her wrist, squeezing tightly, but she didn't let go.

She closed her eyes and then quickly opened them as she gasped for breath. The lines on her face softened and the hard scowl that seemed forever etched into her face melted away.

"I can't stay in the Community," she said softly. "Once the elders find out what's happened to me, I'll be the next one tied to the Burning Tree."

"What are you talking about? What's happened to you?" I asked.

Alison stood up. "I might as well show you. I can't hide it much longer anyway." Alison pulled off her jacket and slid one of her overall straps off. With only a thin white T-shirt covering her stomach, I could see her protruding belly.

"I'm pregnant... with Patrick's baby."

I suddenly felt lightheaded and grabbed hold of the log for support. I had practically begged for her honesty and now could hardly bear the thought of it.

"Does Patrick know? Does anyone else know?" I finally said.

She shook her head and looked down at her stomach. By her own calculations, Alison was about fourteen weeks pregnant and wouldn't be able to hide her condition from Patrick or anyone else for much longer.

***

The week before Easter Sunday, the elders and their wives pored over the Community book, ingesting all the information written inside. It was a time of both anticipation and calm. There were no official meetings, competitions, or sermons as the elders decided who would be coupled together and what marriages would begin by the end of the week. There weren't any activities occurring except for the most basic chores, such as hunting, cooking, and gathering firewood. It was the lull before the storm.

The sudden planning of more than a dozen weddings was supposed to make everyone forget that two girls had been burned to death, slowly and horribly. It seemed to have the intended effect on my mother. She glided through the house as if she were dancing with each step.

"Lace or silk?" she said when I came home from the greenhouse.

"What?" I looked at Abigail sitting next to our mother, meticulously adding fringe to the blanket we had knitted together. Her hands flowed up and down at a regular, even pace, but her face didn't move.

"Do you want your wedding dress made of mostly lace or silk? Lace will be easier to work with, and it looks so pretty. Don't you think?"

I just smiled and nodded. After all, I wasn't going to be here.

The following morning, the entire Community was called into the sanctuary so the announcements could be made.

I sat near the front of the Community Hall, along with the others my age who were part of the Preparation. I watched Alison as she walked in front of where I was sitting, eventually taking a seat on the other end of the bench. She had a large, sloppy jacket over her overalls, hiding her growing stomach.

The elders and their wives sat in a semi-circle behind the podium. The women were wearing bright colors and had wide smiles pasted on their faces. The men wore black and gray suits.

Hayden McVeigh was holding the piece of paper that contained the information regarding who we would marry, bear children with, and spend the rest of our lives growing old with in the desolate Wyoming wilderness.

"After great consideration, we've matched our young people going through the Preparation," Elder McVeigh stated proudly.

He rose to his feet, cleared his throat, and with more enthusiasm than I thought possible, he began reading the names off the list.

"Lynette Brewer and Terrance O'Malley."

I took a slow, deep breath but didn't dare look at Lynette and the look of horror that I was certain was on her face.

"Hannah Sawyer and Brett Stevens."

Again, I breathed in... and out. I was going to be gone. This wasn't going to happen. Several more names were read. When they came to the last couple, I realized that Alison's name had not been called yet.

Did the elders know about her pregnancy? A thousand thoughts raced through my mind. Would they take her baby and give it to a barren Celia and then put Alison to death at the Burning Tree?

"Alison Flowers and Robert McVeigh."

It took a split second for my mind to grasp and understand. Robert? Robbie McVeigh! He was several years older than the rest of us and had been single for so long that I hadn't even considered the possibility that he would now be married.

We were then told to quickly dismiss and return to our homes. The elder's wives would contact those who were engaged and start planning the weddings before the end of the day.

I carefully watched all the others who had recently become engaged as we began to exit the hall. There was hushed chatter, excited whispering, and either joyful expressions or shock and sadness on every face of those going through the Preparation – except for three. Alison, Lynette, and I remained calm and silent, and suddenly, I wondered if anyone else would notice our lack of emotion.

That evening, after the sun had set and Abigail had just gone to bed, I entered my mother's bedroom. She was sitting on the edge of the bed, brushing her hair in the light of the dim kerosene lamp.

I sat down next to her on the bed. "I have to talk to you," I said solemnly.

"I need to talk to you, too," she said, putting down the brush and taking hold of my shoulders. She turned me around so my back was towards her. She took out my ponytail and began brushing my hair. "Your hair is going to be so beautiful once it grows long," she said, bearing down hard with the brush.

"I have to tell you something important," I interrupted, but she wasn't listening.

"I know Brett Stevens was not who you were expecting. To tell you the truth, I was a bit surprised myself."

"It's not about Brett," I said quickly.

"I know, marriage, especially at your age, can be overwhelming."

I opened my mouth again, but nothing came out. I had almost told her about Ross and our plan to leave the Community. But she was too deep in denial. I loved my mother with all my heart, but I couldn't trust her. I couldn't take the chance that she wouldn't tell anyone.

I felt guilty about leaving her behind, but this wasn't just about me. Other people's lives were at stake, and I had to try and save Abigail as well.

I stood up and forced a smile. "I'm tired. I'd better be getting to bed."

# Chapter Twenty-Seven

That night, I barely slept. I was certain my mother slept even less than I had. I had sporadically woken throughout the night. Each time, I peeked out to the kitchen to find her pacing the floor, staring mindlessly out the window, or sitting at the table with her head in her hands.

Each time I saw her like this, I crept back into my room and prayed that the veil of deception that clouded her thinking for so long would finally lift and she'd see the truth. Later, I would realize that I should have also prayed for her mental health. At that time, she was near an emotional and mental breakdown, but my own mental health had been so precarious that I didn't realize how much my mother was struggling.

When I woke that morning, I lay in bed, staring at the ceiling for the longest time. Our life was now in uncharted territory. Even if we managed to leave, I knew all hell would break loose in the Community the moment the elders discovered we were gone. I had no idea what would happen to our families. No one had ever left before. How could I even take a chance and put Abigail in that kind of danger?

I had already told Ross I was taking Abigail with us when we left. Now, I wondered if it was the right decision. I knew it would be dangerous to leave her behind. She would be at the mercy of Jonathon and Hayden. But it could be just as dangerous to take her along. If the elders pursued and caught us, I knew it was likely we would not survive any punishment they deemed necessary to keep order in the Community.

I had to decide whether to take Abigail with us when we left or leave her behind. I had to make this decision alone. No. I was wrong about that.

That's when I crawled out of bed, fell on my knees, and begged God to show me the way. I'd recently spent a lot of time reading the Bible, but prayer was something I struggled with. I wasn't sure how to approach the Almighty Creator, who already knew everything about me.

I simply asked, "Tell me, Lord, should I bring Abigail with me or leave her here?"

I continued to pray, asking God to protect and provide for us. I finished by thanking Him for all His blessings and for sending Ross to the Community.

When I stood up, I didn't sense that I had received an answer. I did, however, sense God's peace and that an answer would come when I needed it.

I came into the kitchen, and through the window, I saw my mother in the backyard hoeing the ground for the garden she would soon plant. Abigail was in the bathroom dressing.

I saw my chance to look for any information my mother had about the extended family we left behind when coming to the Community. I searched the kitchen drawers and the stack of papers and pens she kept in a folder. I found nothing regarding any of our relatives.

I headed to the bedroom to look there. Since we didn't have phones or computers, we kept information in boxes and folders. All our personal papers, such as birth certificates and Social Security cards, were kept in a safe in the Community Hall.

There weren't many relatives I even remembered. My mother's side of the family was from Kansas, and I'd hardly known any of them. On my dad's side, I remembered my grandmother, some aunts, and a few cousins.

I started digging through my mother's dressers. There was nothing there either. The last place I knew to look was a box of old pictures she kept on the floor in her closet. As I opened the box, I tried to think of the names of the relatives on my mother's side from Denver. I remembered Aunt Vicky, and Benjamin, a cousin a few years older than me.

I found pictures of Abigail as a baby, myself in first grade, and one of my dad. Then I saw a picture of a person I knew was Vicky. I studied the picture, trying desperately to remember her last name.

When I heard the kitchen door slam, I quickly closed the box and stuffed the picture into my overalls pocket. I left my mother's bedroom and hurried into my room before she saw me.

I held the photo next to my pillow so no one could see it if they came into my bedroom. I studied the picture of Aunt Vicky sitting on a lawn chair on someone's patio. I used the old trick of reciting the alphabet when trying to remember a name. A... Anderson? No. B, C, D... Denison? No. When I got to H, I suddenly remembered. Vicky Henderson.

Vicky Henderson from Denver was the only relative I could think of to ask for help. Of course, after eight years, her name might not be Henderson, and she might not still live in Denver. But it was the only outside connection I possibly had.

"Abigail!"

Within seconds, Abigail was out of the bathroom and sitting on the bed next to me.

"What's going on?" she asked.

"Shut the door and come back."

After she had done as I instructed, I again brought up Ross.

"Do you remember what I told you about Ross and leaving the Community?" I said, barely above a whisper.

She smiled and nodded.

"You haven't told anyone, have you?"

"No," she said softly.

I knew expecting a nine-year-old to keep a secret like that was asking a lot, but considering what we were living through in the Community, I believed there was no other way.

Before I could say anything else, she leaned toward me and said, "I want to go with you. I want to leave the Community."

This was the answer to my prayer. The fact that she was so certain she wanted to leave convinced me that taking her with us was the right thing to do.

***

That evening, it was dark when Lynette and Alison met me to gather sticks. We had all been occupied with meeting our future in-laws and planning our upcoming weddings. Meeting later, now that it was dark, worked to our advantage, however. It would be easier to go to the cabin and see Ross without being discovered.

He was waiting for us at the door when we arrived. He looked strong and confident. "Hurry, come in."

We all gathered around the small wooden table near the front window.

"We'll leave in two days," he said quickly. "There will be a full moon, and we'll be able to see better when making our way across all the ravines and ditches along the terrain."

"Lynette, aren't you getting fitted for your wedding dress tomorrow morning at Elizabeth McVeigh's house?" Alison said.

Lynette slowly nodded. It was obvious she thought it was strange that Alison would bring that up now.

"Every chance you get by yourself, you need to search for the keys to the van or truck. Hayden likely has them somewhere in the house."

Lynette's face grew pale, terrified at the thought of searching the McVeighs' house.

But Ross intervened before she had a chance to say no. "We can't take the chance that you won't be able to find them, or worse, that you'll get caught looking for them. Besides, I've seen the truck. I'm certain I can start it without the keys."

The three of us hardly spoke at all while Ross laid out the plan in intricate detail. He told us he'd seen the vehicles parked by the barns, far enough from the houses that when he got it started, it was unlikely anyone would hear the engine. He told us we'd leave at two in the morning, giving us plenty of time to reach Cheyenne before anyone in the Community was awake.

All I could think as he excitedly explained his plan, was that Lynette was getting fitted the next morning for her wedding dress. All of us had been scheduled for fittings with one of the elder women in the Community. How in the world would Alison be fitted without anyone finding out she was pregnant? Wearing a baggy T-shirt and thick denim overalls, she could probably hide a pregnancy for several months. But keeping it hidden while fitted for a wedding dress was out of the question.

"I think we should all pray about this so God will watch over us," Ross said. I hadn't even realized he finished discussing his plans. I'd been so occupied with wondering how Alison could keep hiding her pregnancy.

Ross started praying as if it were the most natural thing in the world. He called upon God to watch over, protect, and have mercy on us. The words flowed out of his mouth so beautifully, almost like he was reciting the words of a song. The prayers offered up by the elders in the Community never seemed to surround and comfort me like this one did.

"Amen."

We lifted our heads and looked around the table at each other.

"The day after tomorrow at two am at the barns," he said.

As we walked back toward the Community, our wheelbarrows full of sticks, I couldn't help but ask Alison about her fitting. "So, when is your fitting?" I said.

Alison didn't hesitate when answering, "Mine isn't scheduled until next Monday, with Kathleen Alden."

She knew why I was asking, and she also knew that I was trying to be discreet about it.

"It's a good thing mine is one of the last fittings scheduled since we won't be here anyway."

"That's true," I said. I wondered if Alison had concocted some excuse for why she had to be one of the last to be fitted or if she'd just gotten lucky.

"That's one thing I'll miss about the Community," Lynette said. "Getting a pretty dress and planning for a wedding is fun, even if you don't really want to get married."

"Are you crazy?" Alison blurted out. "Are you going to back out on us, Lynette Brewer?"

"No! I'm just saying, I like pretty dresses, flowers, and planning weddings. That's all."

Alison took over pushing the wheelbarrow and maneuvered it quickly along the path while Lynette and I hung back.

"I'm so scared," Lynette said softly.  "I've been trying to pray to God, but I'm not sure he's listening."

"I don't know much about prayer, but I know God is real. And He's not the angry tyrant the elders tell us He is," I said. "Knowing God is knowing Christ. It's real and it's personal."

Lynette stopped and looked straight at me. "I want to know more. I want to know who Christ really is."

I nodded and put my hand on hers. "When we get out of here, we'll find a good church. We'll study the Bible with people who can help us, and figure out what it all means."

# Chapter Twenty-Eight

I looked toward the greenhouse, realizing that after tonight, it would be the last time I'd ever see it. The nearly full moon illuminated the outline of the curves along the sides of the building.

Of course, I could have a greenhouse and grow a garden anywhere, but I had grown to love my time in this little greenhouse that I'd come to think of as my own. God had given it to me as a physical refuge where I could spend hours away from the rest of the Community while still doing something productive I loved.

Just as I turned my head, I caught sight of a shadowy figure from the corner of my eye. I turned back around in time to see Gretchen heading toward the greenhouse. She hadn't been there in at least a week, and I didn't think she'd come back again until after I had left. I had carelessly left Ross's shirt and dirty plates in the back closet on a table.

I had no idea why she was coming here at this hour. Perhaps she wouldn't go far enough back to see Ross's things. But I couldn't take that chance. I bolted toward Gretchen, ready to make myself a barricade between her and the front door.

"I'll get whatever you need, so you won't have to go inside," I said without smiling too much. I didn't want her to get suspicious. She didn't seem to suspect anything but wasn't impressed with my offer to help.

"Thank you, but I want to get some onions and peppers for a roast I'm making. I also need to get some supplies out of the back closet."

"I'll get them for you," I said, standing firmly in front of her.

"I want to pick them myself," she insisted. "Please move."

"You don't look well. I'll pick them for you and bring them to your house," I said quickly.

I stepped toward her, gently took hold of her arm, and attempted to lead her away from the greenhouse.

She jerked her arm away and began to back up. "I don't know why you won't let me in the greenhouse, but I will definitely report this to the elders."

I was momentarily relieved. By the time she reported me and a meeting was held, I would be gone. If she found any of Ross's things inside, she would have called for the elders immediately. She started to back away, looking at me like she'd never seen me before.

"Just go home, and I'll bring your vegetables to you," I said, acting like nothing had happened.

She kept backing away, moving quicker with each step. When she tripped, she was at least ten feet away from me. She turned to catch herself but landed on the gravel – on her stomach. I rushed to help her, but she fought against me like a wounded animal.

"Don't touch me!" she cried.

She sat up and reached for her knees, but her bulging stomach kept her from getting her hands completely around her legs. She was moaning, crying, and rocking back and forth on the ground. My mind was spinning in a thousand directions. I had to get help and make sure she was alright, and then I would leave.

I started to run, then heard voices coming from the other direction. Someone had already seen Gretchen writhing with pain on the ground. I think it was one of the O'Malley children. I wasn't sure. Everything began happening so fast. Before I knew it, Timothy Lane was running towards his wife while I quickly hid behind the greenhouse.

I watched from the east side of the greenhouse while Timothy Lane picked up his crying wife and carried her to Ruth Anne Weber's home. I remained safely hidden as he carried her away, several children running along after them. I took a deep breath and tried to clear my mind. There was nothing I could do to help Gretchen, and what happened was an accident.

I didn't know how long I stayed hidden. Later, I would think it had to be close to twenty minutes, but I wasn't sure. I just kept focusing on the plan. I would stop at Lynette's and help her pack supplies. After pretending to go to bed, Abigail and I would get up and prepare to leave. We would go to the cabin at exactly two am to meet Ross. He would start the truck, and we would all leave together.

As soon as I was calmed down and had gone over everything several times in my mind, I turned to run toward Lynette's by the back way. I hadn't taken more than a few steps when someone reached out and grabbed me.

"Where do you think you're going?"

I screamed and then instinctively tried to pull away. But Elizabeth McVeigh's grip was firm and her jagged fingernails were already digging into the flesh under my arm.

"I was going to see Lynette." It was the truth, and I said it with conviction.

Elizabeth didn't seem to care whether I was telling the truth or not.

"You're coming with me," she said in a deep voice I'd never heard before.

When I realized that Elizabeth was taking me to her home, I was momentarily relieved. When I saw both Hayden McVeigh and Jonathon Alden sitting at the kitchen table, a fear I'd never experienced before took hold of me. Elizabeth pushed me down into the chair next to Jonathon.

"I was on my way to her home when I found her hiding behind the greenhouse," Elizabeth said sternly.

Hayden McVeigh sat directly across from me while Elizabeth and Jonathon each sat on opposite sides from one another.

It was quiet for the longest time, and I was certain the silence would destroy me faster than their words. Then Hayden

McVeigh began to speak, and I realized how wrong I was. His booming voice and harsh words were much worse than the deafening silence.

"Miss Hannah Sawyer, after the punishments you have endured, I would think that you would have learned the wickedness of rebellion and the evil it brings on our Community."

I started to open my mouth, but the expression on his face told me that he didn't expect or want a reply from me.

"We would have thought, after seeing two of your friends punished at the Burning Tree, you would have come to your senses."

*Punished? That was what he was calling it?*

I no longer had the strength to speak, even if I wanted to. At that moment, I was certain I would be the third girl put to death. My heart was pounding so hard I feared they would hear it pulsating through my chest.

I looked out the McVeigh's window into the moon-drenched night. I instinctively thought about getting up from the table and running. But Jonathan was between me and the front door. There was no way I'd make it past him.

"I think Hannah should lose her place in the Preparation," Jonathon said unexpectedly.

Hayden raised an eyebrow as if he had not considered that possibility. Then he slowly began nodding his head. I had never been so relieved in all my life. Hayden and Jonathon discussed how I would be placed a year behind in the Preparation.

They carried on their conversation as if I wasn't even there. That was all fine and good. Within 24 hours, I wouldn't be anywhere near the Community.

As soon as my heart had slowed back to a normal pace, Timothy Lane came charging through the McVeighs' front door. He stopped and stood behind Jonathon. He slowly pointed a finger in my direction.

"Gretchen lost the baby!" he declared. "Because of her! Because of that witch, our baby is dead!"

***

The death of Gretchen Lane's baby changed everything. There was no more discussion around the kitchen table about punishments that involved anything less than immediate death.

Without a word, Jonathon and Hayden tied my hands behind my back and confined me to the chair I was still sitting in.

"Should I tell the older women to alert the Community?" Elizabeth asked.

While Jonathon tightened the rope around my wrists, Hayden slowly nodded. "It's time we stop this rebellion before it destroys the entire Community," he insisted.

I was breathing quick, shallow breaths while the sweat began to bead on my forehead. In my mind, I could already feel the heat rising like an inferno from the trunk of the Burning Tree.

It took less than thirty minutes for the elder women of the Community to travel from house to house, alerting residents and informing them of what had happened to Gretchen Lane's baby and what was about to happen to me.

I would find out later that Alison had sent Lynette to the cabin to get Ross. Why Alison had not gone herself, I never knew. Maybe she didn't think she could run fast enough while pregnant. Perhaps she decided that if Ross didn't make it in time, she would be the only one with enough courage to fight to save me from the Burning Tree. No matter what the reason, it was Lynette who ran without stopping once and began desperately beating on the cabin door for Ross to wake up.

Ross got Lynette to calm down long enough for her to explain what they had done with me.

"They took her to the Burning Tree! It's happening now!" she cried.

"Okay," Ross said, trying to stay calm. "Let's go. I know what we have to do."

***

Jonathon and Hayden didn't take the time to conduct a trial or plan an elaborate show down the main street of the Community, or even allow me time to see my mother and sister. After everyone was alerted, they put me in the van and drove directly to the Burning Tree.

The entire Community was instructed to march to the north field. Many were holding lanterns and preparing to watch the tree survive while yet another young girl perished in agony.

As I was tied to the tree, I bowed my head and silently prayed, preparing myself as best I could to meet death. When I lifted my head again, I could see the Community standing in groups around me. I could hear the sobs of my mother as she stood nearby, clutching Abigail.

Hayden McVeigh walked toward the crowd. He made a statement about why we were all here and what was about to happen. I didn't remember him doing that when Whitney and Katie had been put to death. Perhaps he had, and my mind, in the shock and horror of it, blocked it out.

"Hannah Sawyer is not only guilty of witchcraft but murder!" he exclaimed, his voice like thunder.

Just as he pulled out a match, ready to light the flame, the sound of an engine roared in the background. I turned my head and could see the Community truck barreling across the field between the Community and the Burning Tree.

The elders stood and watched as the truck drove next to the tree. The strained silence had been interrupted, and confusion and chatter filled the air.

Ross rolled down the window and pointed a gun in the direction of the elders.

I would realize later, that in the confusion of all that was happening, Hayden McVeigh must have been terrified that the authorities had somehow found out what had happened.

Patrick, however, didn't seem to care who Ross was, why he was there, or even that he had a gun. "That's our Community truck you've stolen," he declared. "Get out of the truck and off our land!"

But Ross didn't waver. "Untie her." Ross's voice was calm and even.

Patrick took several steps toward the driver's side of the truck where Ross was sitting. "No," he said.

Ross pulled the trigger and shot into the air. "There are two bullets left, and I won't waste them."

I had never known Patrick McVeigh to back down - ever. But this time, he did. He did exactly what Ross told him to do. Patrick turned around and walked back toward me. While still a few yards away, he pulled out his pocket knife and snapped it open.

For a split second, I thought he might decide to forgo the fire and kill me right then and there. But he used the knife to cut the rope that had me secured to the tree.

As I ran for the truck, nobody tried to stop me. Not Jonathon Alden, Hayden McVeigh, Elizabeth McVeigh, or any of the other elders and their wives. They had to have known if we got away, they would almost certainly face prison for what happened to Whitney and Katie. But Ross's gun, with two bullets left, could have been for any of them, and they also knew that.

"It's time to go," Ross yelled as I climbed into the truck.

When Alison and Lynette ran toward the truck, murmuring began. If anyone else had suspected they would have also tried to leave, I'm certain they would have been stopped. But the element of surprise enabled them to get into the truck before anyone could stop them.

"Abigail!" I cried.

She found the strength to break free from our mother and ran through the crowd. I could hear my mother screaming for her children as we drove away.

## Counselor

For the first time since I've been coming to see my counselor, she seems genuinely shocked at what she hears. She leans forward and places her hand gently on my forearm.

"I thoroughly read your file before your aunt brought you here for the first appointment. There wasn't anything in there about you actually being tied to the tree. I didn't realize you came that close to being put to death."

I nod, and all I can think is how wonderful it feels to sit in the safety of this chair. I can feel the cushion along my legs and up the length of my back, but the stiff bark of the tree against the back of my spine is still just as real in my memory.

"Did you forget that as well? Did you just remember it now?"

"No. I didn't forget it. It was one of the most vivid memories I had when I first came here."

"But you didn't say anything about it. Not to the police or me."

"I remembered, but for some reason, I couldn't bring myself to speak the words out loud."

She types into her computer while I think about what I just said. The memory of being tied to the Burning Tree was one of the last memories of the Community, and my mind had not blocked it out since leaving. Bits and pieces of jagged thoughts swirled in my brain like shattering glass. I don't know if I couldn't put the thoughts together so they could form coherent words, or if saying them out loud was just too painful.

"Are you ready to go on?" she says softly.

I grimace. I'm getting to the part where the elders are chasing us. We're racing across the Wyoming wilderness while being shot at. I take a deep breath, relishing the cool air in the office. I sit up slightly and look out the window. I don't want to go back to the Community, not even in my mind. But I have to go back, at least one more time.

"Yes, I'm ready."

# Chapter Twenty-Nine

Ross slammed the gas pedal and took off across the bumpy field. "Half a tank of gas. We should be able to make it," he said.

"Did you take that gun from the Community? How did you know where to find it?" I asked.

He looked at me and hesitated before saying, "I didn't get it from the Community. It's mine."

I'd find out later he had taken the gun from a police officer when he had escaped from custody. Maybe I shouldn't have felt the way I did, but at that moment, I was relieved he had the gun. And I knew now wasn't the time to talk about it. I turned around and looked at Abigail, Alison, and Lynette sitting in the back seat of the truck.

"I can't believe we're doing this," Lynette said, barely above a whisper.

"I can't believe we were all too cowardly to run away sooner," Alison said.

"I didn't think we would get you out of there in time!" Abigail said. She leaned over the seat and hugged me. Her tears spilled across my cheeks.

"Get back and put on your seatbelts!" Ross ordered.

Ross was an excellent driver, but the terrain was unforgiving, and the truck's suspension was terrible. We had barely gotten our seatbelts on when I looked in the sideview mirror. They were already after us.

It amazed me how quickly the elders returned to the van, readied their guns, and located us. The van was not a faster vehicle than the truck. But they knew the area better than we did. Since they often went into town to buy supplies, the McVeighs and the Aldens knew the wilderness surrounding the Community. They knew the shortcuts, which areas to bypass, and how to catch up to us in only a matter of minutes.

"Do you know where we're going?" I said, looking at Ross.

"The Laramie Mountains are to the east, and Wheatland is to the west. That's all I know," Ross answered.

"I think we've got a few more miles before we run into 500 West to Wheatland," Alison said.

While Ross drove over terrain full of boulders and deep ravines, I was certain our heads would have crashed into the ceiling if we hadn't been buckled in. Even though the elders were still quite a distance behind us, they had already started shooting.

As the first shots were fired, I could hear Ross reciting the Lord's Prayer. It was so beautiful, his rich, low voice filling my head with a sense of serenity. We rounded a sharp corner and suddenly found ourselves in a field behind a thicket of brush.

The first round of shots ended, we were all still safe, and the truck was still moving at full speed. I said a quick prayer, thanking God for protection. Lynette started to cry, and Alison told Lynette to shut up. Praying, crying, and yelling, it all bounced between the walls of the truck as we continued our journey across the ragged Wyoming wilderness.

In the midst of all this, I looked back again at Abigail. Even though she wasn't crying anymore, she wasn't moving or making a sound. It didn't even look like she was breathing.

"We're going to make it," I insisted. She smiled and nodded, but I didn't know if she really believed it.

"You all need to hold on!" Ross yelled. He turned the wheel and headed in a different direction.

For a few seconds, we tried to bend and keep our heads below window level, but being jolted around as much as we were made the effort useless.

"I think we've lost them," Ross said.

His sudden right turn brought us into an area surrounded by trees that provided the perfect cover. There were just enough ash and maple trees with thick, low branches to make it difficult to spot us, but not too many to maneuver between.

For the first time since we'd left the Community, I began to feel safe. A sense of lightness and freedom came over me that I had never experienced in my entire life.

I turned toward the others, still reveling in the thought of imminent freedom, when suddenly, Alison pointed a finger toward my window.

"Look! There they are!"

The van carrying Jonathon, Hayden, and Patrick came flying over a mound of dirt and nearly crashed into the truck as we exited the cluster of trees. Ross slammed on the brakes and made a sharp left turn.

"I don't know the area the way they do. They knew exactly where to cut us off!" he cried.

I turned my head, almost in slow motion, knowing they were right next to us. I saw Patrick McVeigh pull out a pistol and lean across his older brother and onto the open window. With one hand, he held the gun out of the van window and aimed directly at me. With the other hand, he held onto the edge of the open window, bracing himself for the firepower he was about to unleash.

Although I'm certain it only took a few seconds for the following events to transpire, they seemed to last forever.

The moment Patrick pointed the gun in my direction, Lynette let out a blood-curdling scream that nearly pierced my eardrums. Ross slammed on the brakes, causing the truck to fall at least 50 yards behind the van, giving us a few seconds to prepare.

While Hayden spun the van around and came back toward us, Ross leaned across the front seat and did the unthinkable. He moved far enough over to shield me from the incoming bullet. I could feel the impact of the bullet and the powerful thud of his body as it slammed backward, and we were sprawled out along the front seat of the truck.

"Ross is shot!" I heard myself scream.

Alison reached for Ross's gun, aimed toward the van, and fired. The first bullet missed. The second one shattered the front windshield, splattering glass into the van.

"Drive!" I screamed. "One of you has to drive!"

Alison immediately climbed into the driver's seat. I knew she had driven occasionally before coming to the Community, but I wasn't sure she'd be able to do it while being chased.

She didn't have time to think whether or not she could or couldn't do it; she just did it, slamming the gas pedal and breaking through a wooden fence. The fence was in worse shape than it looked, soft and rotten in several places.

I wouldn't find out until much later that the bullets Alison had shot hadn't hit Jonathon, Hayden, or Patrick. But at the time, we didn't know if they were alive or not. We only knew they were no longer following us as Alison drove the van like a madwoman.

As soon as we were away from the direct aim of Patrick and his gun, Lynette and I immediately tried to help Ross. He had crumpled into a ball on the floor of the truck.

"Lynette, help me get him up."

"They're not following us anymore," Alison said. We were now several miles away from where Alison had fired the gun, and she began to slow down.

We tugged and groaned, and awkwardly pushed Ross from the front seat into the back. His body was limp but heavy, and there was blood everywhere. While I remained in the front seat with Alison, Ross was sprawled out in the back between Lynette and Abigail.

"It looks like a shoulder wound," Lynette said. "What am I going to do? He didn't have time to bring anything along except a sweatshirt he had."

"You're going to have to improvise," I said. "Find anything back there you can use to stop the bleeding."

I feared Lynette would crumble under the pressure and that Ross would bleed to death. But she immediately instructed Abigail to start tearing the sweatshirt into strips so she could wrap the wound.

"I can't tear this sweatshirt. It's too thick," Abigail said.

Alison stopped the truck and grabbed the shirt. Once it was torn in several places, she handed the shirt back to Abigail and started driving again.

Lynette ripped Ross's bloody shirt off and began wrapping the strips under his arm and around his shoulder. As she continued to bind the wound, he woke up, and his eyes fluttered.

"What about the bullet? Is it still inside of him?" I asked after she had knotted and tightly secured the wrap.

She shook her head. "The bullet went through the top of his shoulder."

"If the bullet went through him... why didn't it go through me?"

"It's probably in the seat of the truck. Maybe it went through at an angle," Lynette said. She finished the job, and Ross drifted back into unconsciousness. I could hardly believe we had all survived this far.

"We've gotten away!" Alison yelled in a teary voice. It was the most emotion I'd ever heard from Alison in my life.

"We have to stop somewhere, at someone's house, anywhere," I said. "We have to call an ambulance for Ross."

Alison nodded. "And the police. People have to know what's happened in the Community."

I'd temporarily forgotten about Whitney and Katie. The police had to be called. While I was thinking about how good it would feel to know that the McVeighs and Aldens were being led away in handcuffs, Ross struggled to sit up in the back seat.

"Don't call an ambulance." His speech was slurred, but we all understood what he'd said. "And don't call the police, not yet anyway."

"But you've been shot. You need to see a doctor," Lynette insisted.

He shook his head and pulled himself up until he was sitting straight. "I think it's just a flesh wound, and you did a good job of patching me up. As soon as I eat something, I'll get my strength back. There's a diner right outside of Wheatland. Turn right on the next road, and we should get there in about forty-five minutes."

"But I thought you were going to turn yourself in and prove your innocence?" I said.

He took a slow breath. It was obvious how much it pained him just to breathe. "I am, but not yet. I have to see my mom and explain everything. I don't know when I'll get a chance to do that after they arrest me."

I still believed him, even though he could have been lying. For all I knew, he planned to escape and would never turn himself in. But I desperately wanted to believe him, and so I agreed. Alison, however, didn't want to wait to call the police.

"Not call the police? Are you kidding? They've murdered two people. They'll kill more if we give them the chance."

"Give me a few hours. I know someone in Cheyenne. He'll come and get me as soon as I can locate him."

Alison shook her head. "I don't know."

"They're not going to do anything more in a few hours," I insisted.

"You don't know that! They're furious we got away. They're going to take it out on somebody."

I was so torn. I couldn't be responsible for anyone else dying, but if it wouldn't have been for Ross, none of us would have ever escaped. "Ross saved my life," I said. "He shielded me from Patrick's bullet. We wouldn't have gotten away if it hadn't been for him."

Alison reluctantly agreed.

***

I must have drifted off to sleep. I think all four of us did. It was after midnight when Alison pulled into an all-night diner on the outskirts of Wheatland. The lights from the parking lot poured into the side window of the truck, waking me and Lynette.

I turned and looked at Alison. She smiled. It was the prettiest, most natural smile I had ever seen on her face. "We're free," she said. It sounded like she was ready to break out in a joyous laugh. But she was too tired.

Alison was feeling completely liberated while I was overwhelmed. Of course, I was glad to be free from the Community. But there were so many things to do now and so many choices to make. While Ross was snoring in the back and Abigail slept soundly, Alison helped herself to the cash Ross had in his shirt pocket.

"We have to eat," Alison said, fingering through the money. "There's enough for each of us to get a sandwich."

Since I was starving, I didn't argue. I rummaged through the items the elders had left in the back of the truck. I found a large flannel shirt to cover the shirt I was wearing that was stained with Ross's blood.

I would look back later and think how each of us had come into our own that day. What we were to become started under such unbearable circumstances that we couldn't have understood it at the time. Lynette was truly meant to be a nurse. Alison was not as tough as she always pretended to be. And I knew the verse I had recently read was true and trustworthy.

*I can do all things through Christ which strengtheneth me.*

Philippians 4:13

# Chapter Thirty

While the others slept, I stepped out of the truck to stretch my legs and Alison went into the diner to buy sandwiches.

She returned about ten minutes later with ham and cheese sandwiches, bottled water, and a large order of French fries we could all split. I hadn't eaten French fries since I was a little girl, and I gobbled up my portion in seconds.

"Ham and cheese was the cheapest thing on the menu," Alison said.

No one said a word; we were all too busy eating, but I knew we all thought the same thing. This was the best meal we'd eaten in weeks.

When Ross woke up, he covered his bandages as best he could and went inside to call his friend, James. He made up a story about losing his phone, and one of the waitresses let him use hers.

It took about twenty minutes for James to arrive. While waiting, we all sat in the truck.

"I wouldn't be alive if it weren't for you," I said. I wanted to hug him and hold on for as long as I could, but Lynette was busy checking his wound. I could tell by the look on his face that the pain in his shoulder was getting worse, so I took his left hand and held it between my palms.

"God saved you," he said. "He saved us both."

"But you allowed Him to use you. You could have just left the Community on your own," I insisted. "You didn't have to risk your life to help us."

"Are you kidding? You risked your life every day to take care of me."

"So, we're calling the police after Ross leaves," Lynette said as soon as she finished.

I looked at Ross. "That's the plan."

We didn't say much after that, and the time passed more quickly than I anticipated. When an older model Camaro pulled into the diner, I knew this was the part where Ross and I said goodbye. So much had happened so fast that I hadn't had time to anticipate this moment. I forgot all about his shoulder and reached out for him. He flinched but didn't let go.

"I hope I see you again," I said before pulling away.

He nodded. He crawled into the passenger side, and within seconds the car was gone.

After all the things I had been through during the last few months, it was hard to believe that this, in so many ways, was the hardest of all. Perhaps it was just the last in a long line of horrible events, and I couldn't take it any longer.

I had watched Whitney die at the Burning Tree, lost Katie in the same horrible way, left my mother behind, and at least for now, Ross was gone. I knew there was a chance I would never see him again. Just when I thought I would break down, Alison grabbed my hand.

"We're going to make it. It's going to be okay now."

She slowly let go and we headed for the diner. As soon as we were inside, we borrowed a phone from a middle-aged waitress serving biscuits and gravy. She was definitely annoyed that strangers wanted to use her phone.

But we were so accustomed to angry adults that we barely noticed the shocked look on her face when Alison dialed 911 and told the police the short version of our story.

"Are you kids on drugs or something?" the waitress asked as soon as Alison handed back the phone.

Alison laughed. "It might be easier if we were."

The waitress leaned her heavy frame over the counter. "You've been sitting out there in that truck with that Black dude for over an hour, and you're just now calling the police? Wait a minute. Did that guy do something to you guys?"

"He saved our lives," I said. "It's a long story, and you probably wouldn't believe it anyway."

We walked back to the parking lot. That's when it hit me like a brick wall. What if the police didn't believe us?

I turned toward Alison. "What if the authorities don't believe us? Would you believe what we're going to tell them, coming from a bunch of teenagers with a stolen truck?"

"We've got proof!" she yelled back. "The Community is still out there. There are buried bodies out there. The Burning Tree is out there!"

I could hear the faint sound of sirens approaching. "They're coming," I said.

I crawled into the truck next to Abigail. "What's going to happen to us now?" she asked.

"I don't know, but I promise, at least we'll be together." That was one promise I didn't know if I could keep.

The sun had risen by the time we had finished telling the Wheatland Police what had happened, less than an hour from their quiet little town.

During the first few days, we were all examined by psychiatrists, counselors, and doctors. We stayed in a segregated wing at the State Children's Facility. Reporters and television crews repeatedly asked to interview us, but the county officials wouldn't allow it. Thankfully, I was able to keep my promise to Abigail. We were allowed to stay together in the same room.

The night we had escaped, only hours after our interrogation, the state police and two SWAT teams swarmed the Community. Every remaining member was taken into custody, and an investigation into the deaths of Whitney Crouse and Katie Watson was opened.

As the days went on, I would hear bits and pieces of what was happening. The counselors would only allow us to receive fragments of information. A whirlwind of events occurred during the days and weeks that followed our escape from the

Community. This is what we found out during the few weeks that followed:

**The Community:** Except for the elders, most of them would not be held accountable legally for what happened. However, most have no money, resources, or anywhere to live. The Community is considered a crime scene, and they have been ordered to evacuate. No one owns any land or equipment except Hayden McVeigh and Jonathon Alden. Since they have been arrested, the property and bank accounts have been confiscated. While many families are trying to connect with relatives and friends to find a place to stay or secure a job, they are told not to leave the state. They're all to be present as witnesses for the upcoming trial. I have no idea how they will manage to live and support themselves.

**Jonathon Alden and Hayden McVeigh:** So far, Jonathon and Hayden have been the only ones from the Community arrested. They continue to be defiant, insisting they have done no wrong. They are each being held in solitary confinement in the county jail while awaiting trial for the murders of Whitney and Katie.

**Robbie McVeigh:** As soon as the police surrounded the Community, Robbie pulled out a pistol and shot himself in the head. He died instantly.

**Patrick McVeigh:** No one knows where Patrick is. He disappeared less than an hour after Ross helped us escape. He left his wife behind, and a fourteen-year-old girl is missing from the Community.

**Alison:** Alison has been cleared to live with a cousin in Chicago. Since she's still underage, her parents have asked the courts for her to remain with them. However, all parents in the Community have temporarily lost custody of their children. The last I heard, Alison is expecting a baby girl.

**Lynette:** Lynette is being sent to live with her father and stepmother in Wichita, Kansas. She has several siblings she never knew about.

**Ross:** The morning after we escaped, Ross did exactly as he said he would. He went to see his mother and then turned himself in. My counselor told me that after everything came out about how he risked his life to save us and even took a bullet for me, the prosecutor offered him a plea deal that included six months of jail time. His brother Robert confessed to the murder of the woman at the convenience store.

**Hannah's Mother:** Abigail and I have seen our mother a few times for fifteen-minute supervised visits. She is devastated because of what happened in the Community and that she has temporarily lost custody of her children. She is currently undergoing intensive counseling.

**Hannah and Abigail:** My sister and I stayed together at the County Children's Facility. After a week, we were released to the care of our Aunt Vicky. We are both registered to start school in the fall in Denver.

# Counselor

"I think that's enough for today," the counselor says. "Your aunt and uncle are waiting outside."

I nod and sit up. While the counselor types into her laptop, I take a deep breath, thankful I made it through another session. I should know better than to breathe in too deeply. The scent of the Burning Tree is still buried deep in my lungs.

Every once in a while, when I start to lose myself in the past, I hyperventilate. I suck air into my lungs so fast that I'm certain I can still smell the ash and the flame from the north meadow. I can hear the screams of young girls who died slow, excruciating deaths.

But my identity is now in Christ, not any community or group. It was true what so many people had told me, that true peace with God was a relationship, not a religion.

I remember the first verse my new pastor read to me. Psalm 46:10, *Be still, and know that I am God...* And I know, because He is God, that somehow I will not only survive, but be victorious.

# ABOUT THE AUTHOR

Besides *The Burning Tree,* Staz has written several middle grade books, including *Almost Normal, Mrs. Mercutrode,* and *The Last Drop.* She's also the author of *The Weirder the Better,* a middle grade novel published under the name Stasia Decker-Ahmed by Black Heron Press. Links to her books can be found on the website stazbooks.com.

If you have read *The Burning Tree*, Staz would be grateful if you would consider leaving an honest review on Amazon.